JACK IN THE BOX
A DEAD COLD MYSTERY

BLAKE BANNER

RIGHTHOUSE

ISBN-13: 978-1-63696-016-6

ISBN-10: 1-63696-016-2

Cover design by: Damonza

Printed in the United States of America

www.righthouse.com

www.instagram.com/righthousebooks

www.facebook.com/righthousebooks

twitter.com/righthousebooks

PRAISE FOR THE DEAD COLD SERIES

Here are some of the over 100,000 five star reviews left for the Dead Cold Mystery series.

"Rex Stout and Michael Connelly have spawned a protege."

AMAZON REVIEW

"So begins one damned fine read."

AMAZON REVIEW

"Mystery that's more brain than brawn."

AMAZON REVIEW

"I read so many of this genre...and ever so often I strike gold!"

AMAZON REVIEW

"This book is filled with action, intrigue, espionage, and everything else lovers of a good thriller want."

AMAZON REVIEW

DEAD COLD MYSTERY SERIES

ONE

It was spring, and all the trees that had been cold and naked during the long winter were now responding to the watery, early sun by sprouting small, succulent, bright green leaves. The air was chill, but I had the windows of my ancient Jaguar open, and Dehan, in her black leather jacket, was watching me through her aviators as the spring air whipped her black hair across her face. I glanced at her and smiled. She was a nice thing to smile at.

She spoke, outlining the facts.

"Thursday, October seventh, 2014. Helena Magnusson, thirty-five, drives to Underhill Community Center in the Bronx to teach her creative writing evening class. When she gets there, at five thirty, a parcel arrives for her by special delivery. When she opens it, it contains her husband Jack's head."

"Huh! Jack in the box."

"Don't interrupt. Jack Connors, fifty-two, mega-successful founder and CEO of Connors Communication, an advertising company that claims it specializes in 'persuasion engineering,' apparently a branch of neurolinguistic programming."

"Thinking outside the box."

"Are you done?" I nodded. She went on. "The ME said that

his head had been severed with exceptional precision in a single cut. He believed a razor-sharp samurai sword might have been used, or something of that sort. Blood residue on the neck tissue suggested that the man had been lying down when he was decapitated. He also detected traces of ketamine in the blood, suggesting he may have been rendered unconscious before being killed."

"But his eyes were open."

"Yes. So if he was drugged, he woke up before he was killed. The face was tested for fingerprints but none showed up. The rest of the body was never found, despite an extensive search of parks and rivers. What's left of him is probably in the East River somewhere."

"Not habeas corpus, but habeas caput."

"Caput?"

"Head."

"You're on fire today, Stone. Pretty much the only person to benefit from his death was his wife, who inherited a controlling share in the business. Apparently she later sold some of those shares in a private deal to Seth Greenway, the current CEO, and became a sleeping partner. She also inherited a brownstone beside Morningside Park, a weekend house outside New Haven, and another apartment in Boston. She used to lecture there in English literature. Financial gain does not seem to be much of a motive in her case, however, as she was already a rich woman in her own right, being *the* Helena Magnusson."

"Best-selling novelist of dubious talent. You say 'pretty much' the only person to gain from his death. Talk me through that."

"One day, Stone, you will actually read a case file from cover to cover."

I arched an eyebrow at her. "The day you do, perhaps."

She ignored me. We had come to Morningside Avenue. I turned left, and after four blocks, I turned left again into West 122nd. I pulled in between a green ash and a hydrant, killed the engine, and turned to Dehan. She took a deep breath and said:

"The only other person to benefit from his death was Seth Greenway."

"The current CEO."

"But I don't really buy that, Stone. I mean, how sure could he have been that he would get to take over?" She shrugged. "The big problems in this case, as always in a cold case, were a lack of forensic evidence and witnesses, but the lack of apparent motive was also a major stumbling block. Everyone, friends and work-mates, agreed that Helena and Jack were the ideal couple and very much in love with each other, and at work everyone said Jack was a great boss."

I stuck out my bottom lip and grunted. "It's a very striking way to kill somebody, isn't it—severing the head. You can't get much more final than that."

She nodded. "It sends a message, as does putting it in a box and sending it to the wife."

"Almost," I said, "as though *she* were the killer's real target, not the husband."

"That had struck me. But a target for what, exactly?"

"Okay, let's go and talk to her."

We climbed out and made our way down the leafy, Victorian street that, in the age of baseball caps, cargo shorts, and smart-phones, had somehow managed to retain some of its old grandeur and elegance. Hers was the second of a row of understated, three-story brownstones. It had a stone stoop with a magnificent balustrade up to equally magnificent heavy brown doors under a vaguely Egyptian-looking portico. I rang the bell and waited while Dehan went up on and down on her toes a few times, chewing her lip and scanning the facade.

"What do you reckon, three million?"

I glanced at the other houses down the street. "Three, three and a half."

The door opened to reveal a smiling woman in her early twen-ties. She was wearing what appeared to be a surgeon's coat and had very blond hair and very blue eyes. Her voice was fruity and fluty.

"Hello, you are detectives who are calling earlier?"

We showed her our badges and Dehan said, "Detectives Dehan and Stone, we are here for Mrs. Magnusson."

She did a funny little bob with her knees and said, "Yoh, she is expectink you. Please follow."

The entrance hall was unexpectedly large. The floor was an intricate mosaic of hexagonal black and white tiles, with a deep, oxblood Persian rug thrown over it any old how. Large walnut doors stood closed on our left. Beyond them a broad, carpeted staircase rose to the second floor. To the right, a passage disappeared toward what I assumed was the kitchen.

We followed the blond girl in the surgeon's coat up the stairs and along a landing carpeted in the same oxblood red to a second set of walnut doors at the front of the house. There she knocked and went in.

"Madam, the detectives are here."

She waited for an answer we did not hear, then bobbed and smiled at us. "Please come in, yoh."

We went in and she closed the doors behind us. We were in a large drawing room with a magnificent bay window overlooking the street below. The floors were hardwood, strewn with Persian rugs, and the furniture, which was eclectic, seemed not to include anything later than the 1930s. A soft leather sofa sat opposite an iron fireplace, flanked by heavy lamp tables, and on either side of the fire there was a Chesterfield armchair. The paintings on the walls looked like minor impressionists, but they were originals.

Helena was standing by the sofa with her hands clasped in front of her. Her eyes were pale blue, and a small crease between her brows was the only expression on her face. A small frown for a small worry. Her hair was not so much tied up in a bun as tied up out of the way. Her cardigan, the same blue as her eyes, was somehow more noticeable than her pearls. Her shoes, like her skirt, were sensible. She did something with her mouth that, had she ever given it life, might have become a smile.

"Detectives," she said, as though she were considering the word.

We showed her our badges and Dehan spoke. "Mrs. Magnusson, I am Detective Carmen Dehan, and this is my partner, Detective John Stone."

Before she could continue, Helena gave her head a small shake. "You said on the telephone you wanted to talk about Jack . . ."

There was the faintest hint of an accent: a softening of the *t*s and *d*s, a narrowing of the vowels. I wondered if she was Norwegian or Danish. She gestured at the chairs. "Please, do sit down. Have you found something?"

We sat, and she sat almost perched on the edge of the sofa, with her knees together and her ankles to one side, her hands folded on her lap. Dehan shook her head.

"I'm afraid not, Mrs. Magnusson. My partner heads up a cold-cases unit at the Forty-Third Precinct. We periodically review cases that stalled for one reason or another, and we are having a look at your husband's case. I know it's distressing, but we were hoping you could talk us through it."

She raised her eyebrows and gave a little sigh through her nose. "There is so little to tell. I was teaching at Underhill Community Center." She glanced at us, as though realizing suddenly the statement needed an explanation. "So many people, not just young, but mainly older people, in boroughs like the Bronx, never have the opportunity, you know, to express themselves artistically." Her eyes drifted. "Most have nothing to say of any value, but sometimes, you know . . ." She looked at me and smiled. "Not often, you meet somebody with talent. After the class, my publisher was organizing a party at the Chadwick and Holstein offices in Manhattan; we were launching the new book. 2014, let me see . . ." Again her eyes drifted away, as though she were looking at hidden images within the wall. "*The Many Colors of Snow.* My husband was going to pick me up to take me there, but he called, um, one o'clock, about, and said he must come later. He was always so busy at work. So, I took my car. I was always a little early to the class, to prepare, and the young man came to my class . . ."

"Young man?"

"From UPS, I think. He gives me the box, asks me to sign for it, and leaves. I was of course very curious to see what . . ."

She seemed to freeze. Her gaze shifted to the rug, and she blinked several times in rapid succession. It was the only sign that she was feeling any kind of emotion. After a moment, she swallowed and said, "You know, it is such a long time since I have spoken about it. You would think . . . But, in any case, I had not ordered anything, I was not expecting anything, so naturally I was curious. So I opened the box and inside was a cool box, like for a picnic. I took it out, more curious now, and I opened the cool box."

Again she stopped, looked away, and bit her lip. She gave her head a small shake. "He was on his back, as though he was lying down. I have seen him like this more times than I can count, in the morning and in the evening. And he was staring right at me. He looked serious, a little surprised. Very . . ." She frowned at Dehan and ran her fingertips softly over her own cheek. "Very pale, because he had no blood in him. Of course he could not see me. I am told that I screamed, but I don't remember. I remember, the next thing, that I was in a chair, there were a lot of people, and somebody was giving me water from one of those disgusting plastic glasses. I didn't drink it. I could not drink it from such a plastic glass."

She took a deep breath and looked back at Dehan. "The police came, a doctor came, and some paramedics. They wanted me to go to hospital, or at least go home. But that is not the way we do things."

I smiled. "We?"

She met my smile with one of her own that was a little distant.

"In my family. My father was a very strong man. He taught me that we see first to our duties, and we express our emotions later, in private."

"So you went to the book launch?"

She nodded. "Yes, of course."

Dehan scratched her head and left a few stray hairs standing slightly on end. "Mrs. Magnusson, when was the last time you actually saw your husband?"

"At breakfast. We are both early risers, well, he was an early riser, and we always breakfasted together at six. Then he went to work and I went to my office. I work, naturally, from home."

I asked, "And the next communication you had with him?"

"At one o'clock, when he called to say he could not collect me from the community center."

"That would be his lunchtime?"

She looked a little surprised. "I imagine so, Detective Stone. Is that important?"

"I don't know. What did you do after you received the phone call?"

"I had lunch with some friends who were visiting from Boston, some fellow lecturers." She sighed and closed her eyes for a second. "One of them was a friend. The others were friends of his. The details are in the original statement I gave the police at the time."

"Did you go directly?"

She didn't answer for a moment and seemed to be remembering. "Yes," she said at last. "They were already here. I told them Jack would not be coming to the launch and we went. Again, I did tell the police . . ."

Dehan nodded. "I'm sure the detective at the time asked you all of this, Mrs. Magnusson, but sometimes time and reflection can cast a new light on things. Is there anyone you can think of, however remote or unlikely it may seem, who could have had a grudge against your husband?"

She smiled. It was an odd smile that seemed to suggest that

Dehan's question was somehow absurd. Her gaze drifted and she pointed at my chair. "He used to sit there, smoking a cigar in the evening. He liked cognac, the Rémy Martin Fine Champagne, XO . . . extra old." She made a disparaging face and gave a small laugh. "I think it is a vulgar drink in a vulgar bottle, but he likes it . . . He liked it." She took a deep breath and the laughter faded from her face. "Of course, I have asked myself this many times. Who? Who would want to do this? But I cannot answer that question. So many people in his life I did not know. I knew nothing of his work. In his personal life I can tell you that he had no enemies—few friends, but no enemies. At work . . ." She gave a delicate shrug. "I do not know. You would better ask Seth, and his colleagues."

Dehan nodded again. "Sure, we will do that." She hesitated a moment, then said, "Mrs. Magnusson, there is an outside possibility that you, and not your husband, were the focus of this attack. Had that crossed your mind?"

She blinked, and her eyebrows rose a fraction. "What on Earth can you mean?"

"My partner and I both agree that the fact that so much care was taken to send . . ."

She hesitated again, and Helena supplied the missing words: "My husband's head."

"Yes, the fact that so much trouble was taken to send it to you in that particular way suggests that you were, at least to some extent, a target in this crime."

"That had never occurred to me. It is obvious now that you say it, and I a crime writer . . ."

For a fleeting moment her bottom lip curled in, and she blinked away tears from her eyes. I said, "You were too close to it."

"No doubt."

"But you see that there was an attempt here to communicate something to you."

"Yes."

"This would suggest that the murderer knew you both, and considered himself . . ."

"Or herself."

"Yes, or herself, to have some kind of relationship with you. Seen from that perspective, does anyone come to mind? Can you think *what* they might have wanted to communicate?"

She shook her head, not in negation but as though daunted by the enormity of the task. "I shall have to think about it. I have not thought about this for a long time."

I nodded. "Of course. Mrs. Magnusson, I only have a couple more questions for you and then we'll leave you in peace. How did you get from the community center to the party on Madison Avenue, in Manhattan?"

She stared at me for a long moment.

I frowned. "I'm assuming you didn't drive."

"No, no, of course not. A friend from Boston came and picked me up."

I smiled, and my eyebrows told her I was surprised. "From Boston?"

"No, Detective, he was visiting for the book launch. He is an old friend."

"This would be one of the friends you had lunch with. May we have a name?"

Her face seemed to dry and harden like plaster. "His name is in your original report. Do you need to trouble him again after all these years?"

"In a case like this, where there is no forensic evidence and there are no witnesses, we need to gather evidence from other sources. Often a simple comment can give us a clue that leads us to an answer. I am sure your friend is totally innocent, but he may know the killer without realizing it. We are trying to catch a murderer, Mrs. Magnusson, not cause you problems."

"Of course." Again the small sigh through her nose and the downcast gaze. "His name is Alornerk, Alornerk Smith. It is in my original statement."

Dehan frowned. "That's a very unusual name, Alornerk."

"It is an Eskimo name. He is from Alaska. He lives and works in Boston. He is a senior lecturer in mathematics. I believe he has changed address since . . ."

Dehan wrote down his new address and phone number. When she was done, I said, "One last thing, could you supply us with a list of your students at Underhill?"

She sagged back in the sofa. "Now?"

I shook my head. "No, but if over the next day or two you could give it some thought and write down everything you can remember about them, that would be helpful."

She gave a nod that was weary. "Yes, very well, Detective Stone, I'll do what I can."

I glanced at Dehan. She shook her head that she had no more questions and we stood. Helena rang a bell, and we stood in awkward silence for a moment. Then Ebba opened the door and led us back down the stairs in a silent procession to the front door. There she smiled her bright smile and said she hoped we would have a lovely day.

The door closed, and we walked without talking back to my old, burgundy Jaguar, where it sat in the mottled spring shade of the green ash.

TWO

DEHAN DIDN'T GET IN STRAIGHTAWAY. SHE LEANED HER forearms on the burgundy roof of the car, leaned her chin on her forearms, and drummed her fingers. The dappled shade of the leaves lay across her face.

"In her original statement, she said that Alornerk came to visit and brought a couple of friends with him. She couldn't remember their names, but they were visiting from Europe. She couldn't remember the name of the restaurant either. She had never been there before and Alornerk's friends had chosen it, somewhere in Queens."

I listened to her, then unlocked the car door. "You think she's lying?"

She drummed a bit more, then looked up at the young leaves in the green ash overhead. "It's messy and unlikely enough to be true. It could also be a phony alibi."

I climbed behind the wheel, and she got in the other side. I asked, "What did Alornerk say when they interviewed him?"

She frowned at me and slammed the door. "Read the report sometimes, Stone. That's what it's there for."

"I did, bits. I like to keep it fresh. Besides, I have you to read it for me. I like the way you tell it." The big old engine growled and we pulled away. "What did he say?"

She sighed. "He confirmed her story. The friends had gone back to Europe that evening. It had all been a big shock. He couldn't remember the name of the restaurant either. He would contact the friends and get them to tell him. He never did, and neither of them was ever a suspect, so it wasn't followed up."

I turned into Manhattan Avenue. "You want to go and see Seth Greenway?"

"Of course. Fifteenth floor, 667 Madison Avenue. It's in the file."

"Don't judge me. My father used to judge me. That was what led me into a life of dissolute vice and profligacy, and ultimately self-recrimination and self-loathing. It took years of therapy and analysis to make me the man I am today. But the shadows are never far away. The shadows . . . and the nightmares."

She watched me say all this from behind her aviators, with a small smile on her lips. When I'd finished, she said, "You know all about my family, my history, my childhood, but you never talk about your own past, or your parents."

I shrugged. "Not much to tell. My father was an Austrian sadist with a small moustache and blond eyelashes. He used to pronounce Austria 'orstria.' That always terrified me."

She laughed. I smiled. After a bit I said, "Helena made the point that the killer could be a woman. You think that's significant?"

She shrugged. "I noticed that. I don't know. If she suspected a woman, why not say so? Also, ninety percent of murders are committed by men. So, statistically, it's not likely."

"Statistical probability is a misleading friend, Dehan. Statistically, he is very unlikely to have been murdered in the first place, and yet he was."

"Still, I noticed the comment but personally would not attribute much significance to it."

I made a left and a right onto Central Park West and was

temporarily distracted by the beauty of the grass and the trees in the early spring light. At West 97th I turned into the park. "Would you say she was pedantic—in her speech, I mean?"

She thought about it for a moment. "Yeah, I guess so. She's very precise. You get the feeling she was taught extremely correct English and sticks to the rules."

"I noticed she uses 'shall' in the first person."

She frowned at me. "What?"

"Not many people know that shall is the first person of will: I shall, you will, he will, it will." I glanced at her and went on. "We shall, you will, they will."

"You're kidding."

"She knew that."

"Huh . . ." She frowned again. "Is that important?"

"Well, it makes her question a little more significant, because presumably she knows that in English 'he' is a neutral pronoun as well as a masculine one. That may not be popular in our politically correct age, but she struck me as a woman more concerned with propriety than political correctness. I may be wrong, but I think *she* thinks it was a woman."

She shook her head as we turned out of the park and onto Museum Mile. "One of these days, Stone, you are going to come out with one of these gossamer-thin deductions of yours, and it will be totally wrong."

I snorted. "See? And then you want me to share my thoughts. So that you can erode my ego with cruel, stabbing words, like my mother when she used to make me lie under the floorboards, with the rats."

"You're out of your mind, Stone."

"I must have spring fever."

Five minutes later, I made two lefts onto Madison Avenue and parked outside J. Safra. Dehan opened the door to get out, but I sat drumming the walnut steering wheel and staring at the FedEx van in front of me.

"What?"

"The killer knew where she would be at that time, so he could organize the special delivery."

"Yes."

"He also knew Jack was going for lunch."

"Yup . . ."

I eyed her face a moment. "So, where did Jack go for lunch?"

"Let's find out."

"Yeah . . ."

I climbed out and we made our way along the sunlit sidewalk toward 667 Madison Avenue.

We crossed the echoing, toffee-colored marble lobby to the bank of elevators along the far wall, which still evoked Orwell's art deco vision of the future. There, we took a car to the fifteenth floor, in uncomfortable intimacy with a dozen other people, all trying hard to pretend it was normal to be this closely confined with a dozen strangers in a steel box fifteen stories in the air.

The doors slid back, and we exited with relief into the reception of Connors Communication. Here the walls were also marble, but of a pale oxblood hue that was oddly unsettling. A girl who had the kind of charm you learn at customer service school gave us a pretty smile and asked how she might help us.

I showed her my badge.

"I am Detective Stone. This is Detective Dehan. We are investigating a homicide, and we would like to see Mr. Seth Greenway."

She made a call on the internal phone, and two minutes later, a young man in shirtsleeves with hair that looked as though it had been sneezed on came hurrying out of a passage and asked us to please follow him. We did, along a beige-carpeted corridor to a large mahogany door that was guarded by a large mahogany desk. The boy with sticky hair dropped behind the desk and picked up the internal phone.

"Mr. Greenway, the detectives are here . . ."

He hung up, flicked his eyes at us, and said, "You can go right ahead, through that door."

Dehan raised an eyebrow at him. "Don't get up, junior, I'll get it."

She opened the door and we went in.

Seth Greenway was seated with his back to a floor-to-ceiling, panoramic view of New York City, giving the unsettling feeling that he might at any moment fall backward into empty space. The office was minimalist, with a round table and twelve chairs to one side, hardwood floors with rough-woven mats, and furniture that had that Scandinavian feel which reminded you that comfortable was not the same as cozy.

He looked up from a dozen glossy prints on his desk and stood, smiling at Dehan, holding out his hand as we crossed the room.

"Detectives, forgive me, we are rushed off our feet at the moment with deadlines and the rest of it!" He laughed. "Much like any other time! Please, take a seat."

He glanced at me to include me in the offer to sit and looked back at Dehan with a quizzical frown. "You are investigating a homicide . . ."

I said, "This is a cold case, Mr. Greenway. The murder of the former CEO of this company, Jack Connors."

He flopped back in his big black chair, his mouth sagged a little, and he looked back at Dehan with an oddly reproachful expression. "But that was, oh . . . five years ago."

I answered, even though he was still looking at Dehan. "There is no statute of limitations on homicide, Mr. Greenway. We take a murder committed five years ago just as seriously as one committed this morning."

"Of course!" He glanced at me, spread his hands, and looked back at Dehan. "How can I help?"

She didn't answer. I said, "How well did you know Jack Connors, Mr. Greenway?"

He gave a small shrug. "I probably knew him as well as anybody did. He wasn't really one for sharing his feelings, you know . . ." He laughed at the thought. "He was very much a man's man, a man of action. He was all about getting the job done, pulling in the clients, making the next million. He didn't have time for what he called emotional horseshit." He held up both hands, laughing, and spoke to Dehan again. "I'm not saying I agree. I am just telling you the kind of man he was."

I saw a small frown crease her brow. I smiled. "Was he well liked at work? How did his employees feel about him?"

"Oh . . ." He nodded at me several times, like I had touched on an important point. Then he turned back to Dehan. "Make no mistake. His staff loved him. He was uncompromising, direct to the point of being blunt, sometimes rude, but always fair and a very generous employer. His staff loved him. He never forgot a birthday, if somebody got married the firm would be there to help out, mortgages, insurance, healthcare, deaths in the family . . . You name it, he was there, rolling up his sleeves, getting personally involved to make sure his staff were taken care of."

Dehan gave a small snort. I rubbed my hand over my chin and said, "I'm more interested in what he would have called the emotional horseshit: his personal relationships, friends, enemies, jilted lovers, old girlfriends . . . Who was he close to?" I smiled again. "We are looking for somebody who would want to kill him."

He held my eye a moment, then made a small, helpless gesture with his hands. "Who was he close to? Me and Helena is the simple answer. And I don't think either of us really *knew* him. I am not being awkward, Detective, but the truth is Jack never really got close to anybody. Friends, apart from me, I am not sure he had any. He had acquaintances who were more or less close, with a small *c*, but I am talking about people on his team, who he saw at work. I am not talking about people he socialized with. What little social life he had was all through his wife. You know she is a successful novelist, so often attends events, launches, galas. You know the sort of thing. He would usually accompany her." He took a deep breath and sighed. "Enemies, jilted lovers, old girlfriends. He must have had them, I suppose, he was certainly a man who was attractive to women, but if he did, he never talked about them."

I gazed out at the vast sweep of Manhattan behind him, with the Ed Koch Bridge just visible, spanning the water. I spoke half to myself: "He never socialized . . ."

"Well," he said quickly, "that would be inaccurate. He *did* socialize, grudgingly, when his wife forced him to."

"What was your impression of their relationship, Mr. Greenway?"

He held my eye and shook his head. "Make no mistake about that, Detective. They adored each other. I have never seen a couple more totally in love."

Dehan spoke for the first time. "How can you know that if he never spoke about emotional horseshit?"

He laughed out loud and his cheeks actually flushed. "He didn't need to talk about it. Whenever you saw them together . . ." He shook his head, searching for a way to express it. "They were both very reserved, neither of them ever made a public display of affection, but you could just see it in the way they looked at each other, smiled at each other, the small touch of the hand. Everybody agreed, even people who barely knew them. They *adored* each other. And she, I hardly ever see her now, but I know, she never recovered from his death. She used to be bright, lively, fun; but since his death she has just faded away. And her writing! It has become so dark!"

I gave a small sigh and rubbed my chin again. The picture I was getting, both from Helena and from Greenway, was almost absurdly detailed and yet told me nothing about the man. I went for the question that had been playing on my mind.

"You say he never socialized unless it was with his wife. So, where did he go for lunch that Thursday at one p.m.?"

For a moment he reminded me vaguely of a goldfish, staring at me with round eyes, his mouth working on unformed words which never made it past his larynx. Dehan said, "Presumably he had a secretary, and a diary."

He scratched his eyebrow and stammered, "Long, long . . . um . . . long since departed, I'm afraid . . ."

"You mentioned a team."

"As I say, that was about five years ago. There was Jean Reynolds, Angie Byrne, Peter Heseltine . . . Those are the names that come to mind. Angie was the graphic designer, Jean and Peter came from backgrounds in CG, animation, special effects, that kind of thing. They all had creative input."

"They still with the company?"

"Oh, yes, they are still with us, we value . . ."

"Could we talk to them?"

He gave a laugh that was more stress than humor. "They are actually engaged in a presentation right now that is worth several million dollars to the company. Let me arrange it and tomorrow, the day after at the very latest, you can sit down with them and have their full attention."

I smiled like someone who wants to be cooperative. "We'd appreciate that."

Dehan scratched the tip of her nose and asked, "Mr. Greenway, who benefited from Jack Connors' death?"

He opened his mouth, his eyebrows moved in various ways, and he blinked several times.

"Ah . . . *Nobody* benefited from Jack's death. Helena inherited a lot of money and property that was, in effect, *already hers*! She inherited controlling shares in this company, *which she did not want,* because she had zero interest in it; and she ended up selling *me* a bundle of shares. So there was no real material benefit there, but she *did* lose a man whom she was very much in love with.

"You are probably thinking that I benefited by becoming CEO, but you're wrong. Jack was planning to take early retirement anyway, and we had already discussed how he was going to transfer the reins of the company to me, and with them a bundle of shares. As it turned out, I had to buy those shares from Helena, so I actually lost money, and also the support and guidance of a businessman who was frankly brilliant. I miss him every day as a guide and a mentor. Emotional horseshit no doubt, but true nonetheless."

I stared at him a moment, chewing my lip and thinking that he sounded sincere. After a moment he spread his hands and said, "Detectives, forgive me for being blunt, but we are up against tight deadlines, and I don't see that I can be much more help to you."

I nodded slowly a few times. Dehan turned to look at me. I said, "There is just one last question, Mr. Greenway. Who was he having the affair with?"

He closed his eyes and sighed heavily. "I don't know, Detective Stone. I believe he strayed a few times over the years. He never talked about it, but there were telltale signs . . ." He gestured at me. "As you noted, going out for lunch, which was totally uncharacteristic, not collecting his wife from college to take her to the book launch. It was atypical behavior and strongly suggestive of an affair. But I cannot swear to the fact, nor do I know who he was involved with."

Dehan narrowed her eyes at him. "Did she know?"

"Helena?" He hesitated. "She is a highly intelligent woman, very deep and very intuitive. I would be very surprised if she didn't know, but I suspect they both accepted it. For him it was a biological need, and she just accepted that that was the kind of man he was."

Dehan raised an eyebrow. "A man's man."

Greenway shook his head. "Don't attack me, Detective. I don't condone what he did. I am just telling you how I *think* they dealt with it. We never discussed it, and I have no idea what went on in their private lives."

There was a tap at the door and it opened. I turned to look. It was a small man in a suit. He was perhaps in his midthirties with a face that was not unpleasant, but not particularly pleasant either. The only way to describe him was to say that he was nondescript. He stopped dead when he saw us and said, "Oh, I'm sorry . . ."

Seth groaned and managed to turn it into a sigh. "Peter, come in, close the door. These are Detectives Dehan and Stone. They are investigating Jack's murder, five years ago."

His eyes were round, with small lashes. He approached, staring from Dehan to me and back again. He said, "Oh . . ." He looked past us then, at Seth, and said, "We finished the presentation. It went really well. The girls and I have been on our feet for thirty-six hours, we were going to go home if that's okay . . ."

"Of course . . ."

I stood. "Mr. Greenway, thank you for your help. Peter . . ." I turned to him. "We'll walk you down. We have a couple of questions we'd like to ask you. It won't take more than a couple of minutes."

THREE

WE TRAVELED DOWN IN THE ELEVATOR WITH PETER and Angie Byrne. Dehan smiled at them and said, "You carpooling? Got far to go?"

Angie, who had merino wool instead of hair, rolled her eyes and said, "I wish! No! It's public transport for us, ay, Peter?"

Peter's eyes were firmly on the floor. "I'm afraid so."

"I'm sharing an apartment on 116th. But poor Peter is all the way over in the Bronx."

"We're going that way, we'll give you a ride. Right, Stone?"

"Sure, I'm right outside. So you guys were both in Jack's team?"

Angie nodded her shaggy head. "Are you investigating his murder? But that was like, what . . . ?" She looked at Peter.

He said, "October seventh, 2014. Four and a half years ago."

"Is that like a cold case?"

I nodded. "How well did you know him?"

She looked at Peter when she answered. "He wasn't easy to know. He was all about the work. He didn't encourage personal conversation . . ."

Peter snorted. "He was loud, rude, bombastic. Everybody here reveres his memory because he was murdered, but the truth is, he was a first-class jerk."

Dehan gave a short laugh. "That's refreshing. It's what I've been picking up all day but nobody has come out and said it till now. Is that a personal grudge?"

He echoed her laugh but shook his head. "Not at all. He was a great employer, and CC is a great place to work, but he was a jerk and an ego freak."

The doors slid back, and we made our way out to the sidewalk. As we approached the car, Peter said, "Jaguars are very unreliable. Especially the older models."

I unlocked the door. "You ever own a Jaguar?"

His glance was resentful. "No."

We all climbed in, the cat growled, and we pulled out into the stream of traffic. I jumped right in. "So it was common knowledge that Jack was having an affair?"

In the mirror I saw them glance at each other. Angie started to say, "I wouldn't say common knowledge . . ."

But Peter cut in. "Yes."

"No, Peter . . ."

"Come on, Angie! He used to talk to her on the phone, right there in front of us!"

Dehan glanced over her shoulder at them. "How can you be sure?"

Peter's voice took an almost hectoring tone. "Because, even though Jack liked to put it about that he was a private, reserved kind of guy, in *fact* he also liked it to be known that he *put it about* in a different way! So we'd be having a meeting to discuss a campaign or a contract or whatever, and he would receive a call, and . . ."

Angie sighed loudly. "Peter! You don't *know* . . ."

"No, listen. Let me ask you something. If you were having an illicit affair, and you were in a meeting, and you *really*—I mean *truthfully* didn't want anybody to know you were having an affair, how would you deal with the call?" He paused, and nobody answered, so he went on, putting his thumb and baby finger to his ear and mouth. "'Hello . . . no, I'm afraid this is not a good time. Perhaps you could call back at seven. Thank you, goodbye.' Or would you stand up, walk away from the table, and in a loud stage whisper say, '*Penelope! I have told you a thousand times not to call me at work! . . . Yes, I love you too, baby . . . I miss you too . . . Look, I'm in the middle of a meeting, I'll call you later.*'"

It was like the butler had just farted while serving the queen her sherry. The silence was like a physical object in the car. I glanced at Angie in the mirror. "Would you agree with that, Angie? Was it like that?"

She sighed again. "Yeah, it was pretty much like that. I mean, he was a pain in the ass, but he was also brilliant at what he did, and a great boss."

Peter rolled his eyes. "The police are not here to investigate whether he was a great boss or not, Angie . . ."

She cut across him. "And also there is the impact on Helena. Have you guys met Helena yet? She is such a sweet, kind, lovely woman. Everybody loves her, and what she does for underprivileged people? Man! You know her salary for teaching creative writing goes straight to charity?"

I asked her, "What impact would it have on her?"

"She was really in love with Jack. Bad enough that he was murdered like that—and being sent his head in a *box*? Man, that is *harsh*! But to know that he was cheating on her as well?"

We had come to East 116th and I pulled in opposite her apartment. Angie went to get out, but Dehan turned in her seat to look at her.

"Angie? That is a sweet sentiment, but it is not a good reason to lie to the cops or suppress evidence. That's a very serious offense. Do you understand that?" Her cheeks colored. Dehan went on. "A man was murdered, and you would have the killer go free so as not to upset the wife? I don't think you thought that one through, did you?"

"No, I guess not . . . I'm sorry . . . I'd better go."

She got out, and we watched her hurry across the road. I did a U, and we continued on our way to the Bronx. Peter was in the mood to talk.

"You know? We get regular seminars in NLP, neurolinguistic programming? It's kind of gone out of fashion now, but Jack was a big advocate, and Seth is too. And one of the main points about NLP is that some people think mainly in pictures, some people think mainly in words and sounds, and some people think with their feelings. That's Angie. Like you said, Detective Dehan, they don't follow through and analyze the consequences and implications of that first feeling. They just allow the feeling to kind of rule them. It was crazy, Jack was killed and there was like an automatic conspiracy of silence to protect Helena."

I frowned at him in the mirror. "You telling me that the whole staff lied to the original investigators?"

He shook his head. "No, nothing so black and white as that. Jack never came out and said, 'I am having an affair,' therefore none of us *knew* that he was having an affair, and as they were both quite obviously very fond of each other, the collective conclusion was that he was *not* having an affair. So nobody lied, but nobody told the whole truth either."

Dehan said, "So, Penelope? Was that her name?"

"Yep, Penelope Peach."

Dehan grinned and looked over her shoulder again. "Penelope Peach? Are you kidding?"

"No, that's her name. It's a hard name to forget. I heard him dictating her name and address over the phone. He was having something delivered to her. I don't know what. I can't remember the address, but it was on the Upper West Side, not far from his own house."

I studied him a moment in the rearview. "You didn't like him much, did you?"

"Not really. I didn't dislike him much either. I thought he was a narcissistic egomaniac, and it kind of annoyed me that everybody bought into his 'firm-but-fair' great guy act." He gave a small shrug. "He was living proof that his system worked. He was a crass, vulgar oaf, but he *told* everybody he was an amazing guy, and they all believed him."

Dehan gave a single nod and pulled down the corners of her mouth. "Is that what persuasion engineering is?"

"It's a little more complex than that, but in essence, yes. It's based on the idea that communication is *always* what the other person understands. If in my language 'I love you' means 'I hate you,' and I say to you, 'Detective Dehan, I love you,' what I have communicated is the opposite of what I actually intended to communicate. My intention plays no part in the communication. Communication is what you understand, not what I intend."

I gave a small grunt. "That's pretty obvious, isn't it?"

"On the surface, perhaps. But then consider that each individual has his own language. Ninety-three percent of all communication is nonverbal. We communicate in hugely complex ways: tone, expression, twitches, gestures, body language—all of which flow from our unconscious urges, needs, fears, and appetites; and all of that complex bundle is our own, personal language. So a skilled communicator takes the trouble to learn the language of the person he wants to communicate to, and tells them what they want them to hear, see, and feel, in *their own language.* Jack was a passed master at that."

"But you didn't buy into it?"

He laughed. "Jack never thought I was important enough to learn my language. Consequently, I saw through him, and he didn't even see me."

"How about Helena?"

We were on the bridge, and I saw him look out of the window at the wide expanse of water. "I think it suited them both to present this image of a united couple deeply in love with each other. I think they really were fond, but I also suspect they had stopped being in love a long time ago."

Dehan had turned and wedged her back against the door so she could see him. "How well did you know her?"

I saw him smile out at the water. Then he turned to face her. "Maybe I could start my own business teaching NLP to the NYPD. Then you might start asking more subtle questions. I didn't know her very well at all. She would sometimes come into the office, charm everyone, be superbly, elegantly European, and then leave. I am not a brilliant observer, there are people at work who are real masters. They call it calibration. They will actually detect changes in your skin texture and breathing pattern while they speak to you. But I'm not that good."

"I read somewhere that NLP is basically a form of hypnosis."

"Not basically, that is exactly what it is. And not *a* form, but many forms. NLP is a range of highly sophisticated techniques for putting people into trance and manipulating their unconscious while they're there."

We were quiet for a while as we drove along the Bruckner Expressway, headed east. As I moved off, onto the boulevard to take White Plains north, he said, "I did try to talk to Detective Langstrum, during the original investigation, but he didn't seem very interested. I guess because everybody else was giving him the official version."

We dropped him outside his house on St. Lawrence Avenue and watched him push through the gate, unlock the white door, and go inside. When he was gone from view, I pulled out and we made our way back toward Story Avenue and the station. Neither of us spoke until I had parked the car and killed the engine. Then I looked at Dehan and said, "I am trying to work out what happened just there."

She nodded. "Me too. Roast beef sandwiches and coffee might help. You go get 'em, big guy, I'll search for Penelope Peach. Like the man said, there can't be many of them."

"Sounds like a plan."

When I got back from the deli and put the brown paper bag on the desk, Dehan was on the phone, sounding sweet and friendly.

"Oh, she's not there right now? But you think she'll be back next Monday? With friends . . . I bet she has! Well, how about you, honey? You sound like you are just *gorgeous*! We have a *superb range* . . . Well what are you *laughin' at*? Nobody ever told you you sound beautiful? Well, I just don't *believe* that!" She reached over and took a beef sandwich from the bag, checked it for pickles, and gave me the thumbs-up. "Okay, honey, well, I'll call back Monday, but you think about what I told you. Bye now!"

She hung up and bit into the sandwich. I said, "I think you derive a perverse pleasure from these personae you adopt."

"Personae?"

"I gather she is visiting friends for the weekend."

She spoke with her mouth full. "Dere a' chew Phenelophe Peash im Mew Ork shtate." She swallowed. "Only one in New York City. Flat A, tenth floor, 464 Riverside Drive. She's in the right class for him to have noticed she existed and engineered some persuasion."

I sat, took a bite of my own sandwich, and asked, "Have we got a picture?"

"Gorgeous. She's an actress, so she has a small presence online."

My phone pinged, and when I checked, she had sent me a picture of a partly clothed woman of prominent charms. I shrugged. "Not my type. Too . . ." I shook my head. "Too too."

"Yeah? I think you're in a minority."

"You got a cell?"

She nodded. "And her GPS is switched on." She pointed at her screen. "She's in Madison, Connecticut. She's at a big house on Lantern Hill Road."

"Dystopia is alive and well."

"You want to call ahead or be all dystopian and just turn up? 'Vee know vere you are! Vee can finet you anyvere unt make you obey!'"

"That sounds like fun, but I think we'll call and see if she's willing to talk to us. If she's not, we can try some persuasion engineering."She tossed me a piece of paper with a number on it. "Something tells me she'll be more responsive to a man."

"You're a cynic, Dehan. I bet she's a really nice person."

I dialed and waited while it rang. After a moment, it stopped, and a voice like the chiming of tiny silver bells said, "Hel-lo-hoo! Penny Peach speaking!"

I inserted a fatherly smile into my voice, avoided eye contact with Dehan, and said, "Ah, Miss Peach, this is Detective John Stone of the NYPD."

"Oh, Lord." A small giggle. "What have I done?"

I laughed. "Nothing that I am aware of, Miss Peach. I head up the cold-cases unit here at the Forty-Third Precinct in the Bronx, and we were hoping to ask you some questions about an old case we are investigating."

There was a long silence. I was about to ask if she was still there when she said, "What case, Detective?"

The acoustics and the sound quality had changed, and I gathered she had moved away to a more private spot.

"This would have been about four and a half years ago . . ."

I left the words hanging, curious about how she would respond. Her response was a half-hearted laugh and, "You're teasing me."

"Do you know what case I am referring to, Miss Peach?"

"I'm not sure."

"If you were sure, what would it be?"

"Was it a homicide?"

"This is not a guessing game, Miss Peach."

"Jack . . . ?"

"Would you be willing to talk to us this afternoon? We believe you might have information that could be very helpful in our investigation. As I am sure you can appreciate, it is vitally important that we eliminate you from our inquiry."

"Eliminate *me*? Am I a *suspect*?"

"Not right now, and the best way to avoid becoming one is to cooperate fully with us. We will be discreet, Miss Peach, and if your relationship with him is not relevant to the murder, it need never become public knowledge."

I heard a small sigh. "Yes, all right, when will you be here?"

"In about two hours."

"Okay, I'll see you in two hours at Cristy's, on Wharf Road. And, Detective, please do be discreet. I am here with my fiancé at his senior partner's house. There is a lot riding on this visit."

I glanced at Dehan and smiled. "I'm John, my partner is Carmen, we're just passing through and we thought we'd look you up. Let's make it the Madison Beach Hotel, we'll be staying over till the morning."

". . . Thank you. That's very . . . sensitive of you. Carmen is a lucky woman."

"See you in a couple of hours."

I hung up. "Well, Carmen, how do you fancy dinner at the Madison Beach Hotel?"

"Do they do bison steak?"

"No, but they do prime fourteen-ounce, twenty-one-day aged New York strip, roasted garlic smashed potato, grilled asparagus, applewood smoked bacon butter, and crispy leeks."

"Sold to the girl with the appetite. Let's go talk to daddy's latest fan."

We stood, and I saw Mo, large and pale with his shirt untucked, staring at us from the next desk across the aisle. He shook his head. "Do you two know how nauseating you are?"

Dehan pulled on her jacket and grinned. "What are you having for dinner, Mo?"

"Get lost."

"Who knows? We might, tramping barefoot along Madison Beach; see where our wandering footsteps take us."

"Yeah," he growled at the papers on his desk. "Here's hoping."

We left.

FOUR

Madison is a small, pretty town that feels as though it has been carefully tucked into a tiny pocket on the edge of an immense forest that stretches far across the continent, from New England deep into Canada. It feels that way because that is basically what Madison is. As we turned into Wharf Road from Boston Post Road, wherever we looked there were trees, thousands of them: oaks, red maple, sugar maple, vast beech trees, and pines, all bulbous and billowing like clouds of green smoke rolling across the landscape; and tucked in among the foliage, dwarfed by it, were houses, steeples, and chimneys, understated and elegant, which were not at odds at all with the wild woods that surrounded them, but seemed to be a part of them.

"I could retire somewhere like this," I said.

"Retire? We have to have kids before you retire."

"Kids, in the plural."

"Two or three."

"I could get myself elected sheriff."

"Then I could raise the kids and bake apple pies."

I smiled. It was a nice image. We cruised gently down past the golf course, and after a moment Dehan grinned. "No, not a sheriff. I think you should become a novelist and write about our

cases. You could be like Jessica Fletcher in *Murder She Wrote*."
She started laughing. "You'll have to wear slippers and a cardigan, and start smoking a pipe."

"Funny. You're funny. The way psoriasis is funny."

We pulled up outside the hotel and climbed out. It was a cute bay with a white sandy beach flanked by rushes and grass, and a row of gabled, New England houses in gray and white clapboard. That was to the north. Behind us, to the south, was a large, elegant, colonial building that was two, three, and four stories high, depending on which bit you were looking at. It seemed to ramble, like an agreeable fireside conversation, with long, white verandas, blue-gray walls, and hexagonal turrets that were almost Chinese.

We checked in, dumped our overnight bags in our bedroom, and went down to find the Wharf Bar. We ordered two Martinis and sat in a booth. Penelope turned up fifteen minutes later, at ten past two.

Raymond Chandler once described a woman as the kind who would make a bishop kick a hole in a stained glass window. Penelope Peach was that kind of woman, only she'd have had him selling the relics too, to pay for her Manhattan apartment. Her big, blue eyes spoke to you of innocence, while her full, red lips told you the innocence was just as skin deep as you wanted it to be. What the swing of her hips told you was all kinds of anything but innocent.

I stood as she came in and approached our booth. Her eyes flicked over me, and I got the impression she'd read me, figured she had my number and knew just how to play me. When she shook Dehan's hand, her expression was more cautious. That was where she thought her problem would be.

She sat beside Dehan, facing me, and the waiter came over and asked her if she wanted the usual.

"No, Sam," she said, like he was the man she'd always dreamed she'd come home to. "Today I'll just have a white wine." When he'd gone away, she turned to Dehan. "It was so kind of you to do this. I don't know what Stephen would make of it."

Dehan shifted into the corner, so she could look at Penelope. "Stephen is your fiancé?"

"He is, and he's a darling, but he is not exactly broad-minded. You know what lawyers are like! Everything has to conform to the rules."

I arched an eyebrow at her. "In my experience, when they are not breaking a rule, they are trying to bend it. Miss Peach . . ."

"Penny, please, we're old friends, remember?"

The warmth in her eyes said that she wished we were. It was a warmth that wanted to be believed and would have been easy to surrender to. I smiled and said, "Right, Penny. What can you tell us about your relationship with Jack Connors, Penny?"

She shook her head. "My goodness, I didn't think anybody knew about that." She laughed and turned to Dehan, laying her hand on her knee. "You must be awful good at what you do!"

We both smiled without much warmth and waited. The laughter drained out of her face. "I'm not proud of what happened." She sat back and laid both hands on the table. Her eyes rested on the diamond engagement ring on her finger. "I met Jack about six years ago. It was at a party in a penthouse some-where in Manhattan. The owner was the director of a big corpo-ration and they were paying Jack some absurd amount of money to promote their brand. I was there with one of the executives of the company. He had proposed to me, and I was seriously consid-ering marrying him. Mark . . . No, Mike. Sorry!"

She laughed like she was more amused than embarrassed. The waiter brought her wine and she made a point of making eye contact when she thanked him. Dehan prompted her, "So you met Jack. Did you meet his wife too?"

"I saw her, but I didn't meet her. We talked for a while, he fascinated me, and I gave him my number."

Dehan didn't try to conceal the edge in her voice. "What happened to Mark, Mike, Micky, whatever his name was?"

Penelope gave a small sigh and held my eye for just a moment too long for it to be comfortable, before turning to Dehan.

"Let me be up front about this, Carmen. I'm a gold digger, and I don't pretend to be anything else. Most of the men I am with like to delude themselves into believing I am something I am not, but I never lie to them, and I never make them promises I can't keep. That's my own code. I am not apologizing, and I don't honestly need your approval."

I stepped in before Dehan could answer. "Penny, we're not concerned with how you live your life or any of its moral implications. We are just interested in Jack, and what happened between you two."

She played with the stem of her glass for a moment. "Jack was about twice my age. He was very successful and very rich. His company was already worth a fortune by then. He called me a couple of days after the party and we met a few times at my apartment in Brooklyn." She smiled at the memory. "He didn't like it —the apartment. He said it was too small and inconvenient. He wanted me somewhere where he could come over at lunchtime. His attitude would have been offensive in anybody else. He made no secret of it: as far as he was concerned, he owned me." She shrugged. "But somehow he pulled it off, and the truth is, I kind of enjoyed being owned by him. He was a rare man, powerful and magnetic. Irresistible."

I said, "So he moved you to the Upper West Side."

She nodded. "It was close to his office and close to his house."

Dehan said again, "So what happened to Mike?"

"Frankly, he wasn't in the same league. I broke it off with him and began to think seriously about the possibility of a future with Jack."

I frowned. "You really think he would have left his wife for you?"

She hesitated, then gave her head a small shake. "No, but he was happy to keep me in style. We never talked about his wife. He gave me to understand that she would never question him. And he wasn't all that interested in what I did, just so long as I was there when he called. It was a pretty good arrangement and a pretty good life."

I sipped my Martini and asked, "Was he the only one? How many other men were you seeing at the time?"

"Two, Stephen and Grant."

Dehan glanced at me. "Stephen?" She jerked her thumb in the general direction of Lantern Hill Road. "The same Stephen?"

"Yes, I had just met him around that time."

"At a party?"

The sarcasm was clear in Dehan's voice, and Penelope sighed. "Your judgmental attitude makes it hard to be cooperative, Carmen. You don't approve of what I did. You've made that clear, but forgive me, that is your problem, not mine." She paused a moment and went on. "I met him walking the dog in the park. He is a really nice guy, and I actually started to have serious feelings for him. I found myself feeling happy at the thought of seeing him and spending time together. More important than that, I found I wanted to make *him* happy." She gave a small shrug. "When Jack died, I was already thinking about breaking up with him, and Grant."

I signaled the waiter to bring another round. "Did Stephen know what you did for a living?"

"No, absolutely not."

"How can you be so sure?"

"Because he would have dropped me like a hot brick. He comes from a very strict, New England Methodist family, and he is very rigid in his morals. Twice he has come close to losing his job with the firm because he has refused to make false statements. He is like *super* moral. If he knew about my past, he would not be with me."

Dehan drew breath, I gave her a look, and she closed her mouth. I said, "Tell me about Grant."

She smiled and shook her head. "Grant was a piece of work. Man, he was something else. He was South African, with this real kind of badass South African accent? He used to pronounce it 'Seth Efrica,' real kind of harsh. He was seriously rich and well on his way to becoming a billionaire. Back then he was, I don't know, thirty-five? And Jack was *poor* by comparison."

Dehan was frowning. "Dot com?"

She shook her head. "No, arms, security, mercenaries. Offices in Manhattan and supplied private armies to warlords in Africa, Latin America, even the Middle East. A lot of it was real shady stuff, but *man* did he pull in a lot of money! Shaw Line Defense is the company."

"He knew how you made your living?"

She gave her head a little twitch to the side. "He'd been around the block a few times. He wasn't exactly naïve, you know what I mean? He knew there were other guys and I depended on them all for the way of life to which I had become accustomed. He didn't like it, but he was coming around to the idea that if he wanted this all for himself, he had to put a ring on it."

I said, "He wanted to marry you?"

"Yeah, we talked about it."

Dehan said, "But?"

"Let's say I was weighing my options." She leaned back to allow the waiter to set another glass of white wine in front of her. Then he set out the Martinis and left. "On the one hand there was Stephen, who I was growing real fond of, then there was Jack, who was generous to a fault, gave me the apartment and stayed out of my hair, and then there was Grant, who was headed for the Forbes five hundred and was willing to marry me; but I was beginning to ask myself what price *I* would have to pay for being his wife."

I asked, "How did you find out Jack was dead?"

"I called his office on the Friday morning."

"You did that a lot?"

"It used to drive him crazy, but it was naughty fun, and secretly I think he liked it."

"And they told you he was dead?"

"His secretary was hysterical. She told me about his wife finding his . . ." She seemed to go slightly pale. "It still makes me sick to think about it."

Dehan sighed and scratched her head. "What were you doing on Wednesday, late morning to early afternoon, Penny?"

"You can't think that *I* . . ."

"I can think all kinds of things, just tell me what you were doing on the Wednesday morning to midday."

She seemed to sag. "Okay . . . I remember it quite vividly. It might sound trite, but I had a hangover. I'd had dinner with Grant the night before and one thing had led to another . . . It wound up being quite a wild night, lots of drink and . . . stuff, big row, makeup sex and booze . . ." She shrugged. "So I woke up feeling rough, to say the least."

She stopped talking and sat staring at her fingers on the table. I drew breath but she started talking again.

"Jack was not crazy like that. He knew everything and was right about everything, and if you disagreed, he just ignored you till you saw sense. But Grant was wild. It wasn't enough that you did what he wanted, you had to agree, and *want* what he wanted too! He was real intense."

"What did you row about?" It was Dehan.

"Exactly what you think we rowed about. I told him I wanted to end it and that there was a man I was thinking of marrying."

"Stephen?"

"Yeah."

"How'd he take that?"

"How do you think? He once explained his philosophy of life to me: take it; if you can't take it, buy it; if you can't buy it, shoot the owner and take it."

I grunted. "So did you tell Grant who you were thinking of marrying?"

"Of course not . . ."

She said it without much conviction and left the words kind of hanging. Dehan said, "But?"

"Well, for about a week or two before Jack was killed, I'd had the feeling I was being watched or followed." She shrugged. "Stalked, maybe."

I leaned forward. "Anything more definite than a feeling?"

"Maybe. A few times I saw the same white van. It was parked outside my apartment on a couple of nights, and when I went for walks in the park, it was there two or three times. I didn't think much of it at the time, and after Jack died, I stopped seeing it."

Dehan scowled at her. "That could be really important. It's a shame you didn't come forward at the time."

She stared at her wine and looked unhappy. "I suppose it is. It never occurred to me at the time."

I gave Dehan a microscopic shake of the head and said to Penelope, "Did you notice anything particular about the van? Plates, logos, any kind of distinguishing feature?"

"No, just that it was white, it was dirty, and it had no windows in the side panels at the back. No logos, no writing. I don't recall the plates."

"Where is Grant now?"

"As far as I know, he still lives in New York. His offices are at 184 Fifth Avenue, above the printers. He has the seventh and eighth floors. They don't look like much from the outside, but he's the real deal. You should see his apartment and his country house."

I nodded. "I believe you. You got a number for him?"

She looked down at her hands and gave her head a small shake. "You better contact him through the company."

Dehan made a question at me with her face. I shook my head. She turned to Penelope. "I have only one more question, Penelope. On any of those occasions when you noticed the van, were you with Jack?"

She didn't answer for a while. She didn't look as though she was trying to remember. She looked more like she wished she could forget. Finally she sighed and said, "Yes. Twice it was parked outside the apartment when he was there. I told him about it, and he dismissed it as silly paranoia." She hesitated just a moment, then said, "Shaw, Grant Shaw."

She took hold of her purse and made to stand. "Is there anything else?"

I shook my head, and Dehan said, "Not for now, Penny."

She stood and left.

FIVE

It wasn't exactly a moon, it was a thin crescent sliver of a moon, suspended a couple of inches above the water: just enough to make the horizon translucent and dapple the inky liquid with a luminous splash. The spring weather was not warm enough for going barefoot, but we wandered along the shore, and Dehan nestled comfortably under my arm, with both of hers around my waist, and we muttered quietly to each other as we went.

"You'd seriously consider retiring to a place like this?"

We paused, looking out at the black bulk of Tuxis Island silhouetted against the pale glow of the moon.

"Why not? It's halfway between Boston and New York, it's one of the safest communities in the country, it's pretty, peaceful." I kissed the top of her head. "Don't you ever get tired of the in-yer-face hostility, and the vast, overpopulated dirtiness?"

She nodded, then looked up at me. "Be a hell of a change, huh? What does a Bronx girl, born and bred, do in Utopia?"

I gave her a squeeze. "I don't plan to retire for a while yet, kiddo. But when the time comes, I can think of worse places."

"Could we buy a boat?"

"Why not?"

"And will you promise me you'll never join the country club or the yachting club?"

"You have my solemn oath."

The delicate smell of cooking reached us through the dusk. A car parked and people climbed out, chatting, laughing. The lazy echoes of the car doors, and the voices, dispersed like chimney smoke on the evening air. We turned and started strolling back.

"I guess," she said, "that men like Grant Shaw, and women like Penelope, are drawn to the big cities, where there are richer pickings."

"This is your way of telling me we are about to talk shop?"

"You know it is."

"Hit me."

"Well, set me right if I am way off, Sensei, but it seems to me pretty obvious we're looking at Grant Shaw as our prime suspect."

I had my right arm around her shoulders. She released her right arm from my waist and took hold of my dangling fingers, then thrust her left hand in my back pocket. We walked like that for a moment, pushing through the sand as she watched her feet.

"It's a pretty classic situation," she said at last. "A tough guy hooks up with a prostitute, they have some kind of chemistry, and he starts to form a dependency. He wants to own her, have her exclusively for himself. He thinks he's in love, but really he just has a violent, emotional addiction. So he tells her he wants to marry her. She says no, and so he either kills her or the guy she's with. It's one of the reasons hookers have pimps."

I grunted and sucked my teeth. She kept on going.

"In this case, our possessive John happens to be a billionaire with a private army at his disposal. He's probably a guy with a lot of self-discipline. So he hires one of his mercenaries to stake Penelope out. His hit man reports back that there is a guy seeing her on a regular basis, so he has him follow Jack and kill him."

"By cutting off his head with a samurai sword?"

We had come to the road and now climbed the steps to the

porch and made our way through the bright lobby to the dining room. There the waiter showed us to our table and handed us a menu each.

"We know what we want," I told him. "We'll have the Prince Edward Island mussels to start with, and then the prime New York strip. And let's have a half bottle of Las Pizarras with the mussels, and a Snowden Cabernet Sauvignon with the beef. You could open that now, to let it breathe."

He gave a little bow and went away. Dehan was watching me with a small smile. "You dig all that, don't you, Stone?"

I shrugged. "My father, he had an interest in wine. He and my mother used to go on wine tasting holidays. He was a good man, a bit cold and distant, but he tried to instill good values in me: honor, honesty, and an appreciation of good things."

"Is there a punch line coming? Is this the 'Orstrian' one with blond eyelashes?"

"No." I laughed. "His ancestors were English, and he really was like that. So, you were going to explain about the samurai sword."

She rolled her eyes. "Okay, well, it's not as odd as it may seem. If a guy like Grant Shaw employs a hit man, there's a pretty good chance he'll be a mercenary of some sort. And a lot of those guys are into the martial arts in a big way. Kendo, Japanese sword fighting, is central to a number of Japanese arts, like aikido, budo generally. So the use of a sword may not be that odd after all."

"It seems a little extravagant. He could have used a suppressed automatic . . ."

She was nodding before I had finished. "Yes, and that would have made sense if he had simply wanted him dead. Then he could have shot him at his house and be done with it. But that's not what happened. He was drugged, kidnapped, and killed while he was awake, by having his head cut off. Clearly the killer—or at least the guy employing the killer—wanted to make a statement."

I nodded, then shrugged, then sat back so the waiter could deliver the Martinis. "All that makes sense, Dehan; what doesn't make sense is that he delivered the head to Helena instead of Penelope."

She sighed at her drink and sipped it. "That is kind of wrong, isn't it? Unless . . ."

Her eyes became abstracted, and she set down her drink carefully, as though she might spill it.

"Unless . . . Okay, this sounds like reaching, but this guy is not only violent, he is also subtle and intelligent, okay?"

"Okay."

"So he wants to send a message to Penelope, but he also wants to claim her as his prize. He wants to own her—marry her. Obviously he knows that if he sends her her lover's head in a box, it's not exactly baubles and bangles and beads. What he needed is exactly the right degree of fear and horror to make her submit without making her run. So he sends it to the wife. That way he gets maximum publicity, ensures Penny hears about it, achieves maximum destruction of Jack's reputation, but maintains enough distance so that Penelope can never be one hundred percent sure if it *was* him, or it wasn't."

"That is subtle."

"Too subtle?"

"No . . . Well, we won't know if it's too subtle until we meet the man and talk to him, but on the face of it, I can see a man going to those lengths for a woman he is obsessed with."

"What other options have we got?"

"Stephen, whom we know nothing about, a number of unknown quantities from her class . . ."

"Yeah, by all accounts she seems to have been a fascinating, captivating woman. It is possible one of her students became obsessed."

"It certainly is. And then there is Helena herself."

"Wow, yup, that is a definite possibility. Only . . ."

"Only everyone says they were deeply in love?"

She nodded.

"The biggest motive for murder known to man. Or woman, as Helena herself pointed out."

"Huh . . . a kind of confession?"

"I don't want to overstate it, Dehan, but it is a possibility. And there is another possibility which we haven't considered so far."

"Penelope."

"Indeed. So far we only have her side of the story. The most convincing lies are the ones that are nine-tenths truth. It is not hard to imagine that everything she said about Stephen was true, except that it wasn't Stephen she was falling in love with, it was Jack. If she was falling for Stephen, why has it taken them almost five years to get hitched?"

"That's true. But wouldn't she have killed Helena instead?"

"Not if it was Jack who rejected her. It almost feels like an act of spite, like a child who is forced to give back a toy she wants to keep, and smashes the toy so that the other child can't have it either."

"Yeah, I get that. Samurai sword?"

"Hmmm, that's tricky, though from a Freudian perspective, it is a pretty powerful symbol of castration."

"Nnyeah . . . no."

"Why?"

"Why not just cut off his balls? If you want to castrate a guy, and you've got something razor sharp in your hands, why waste your time on his head?"

"Fair point."

An ice bucket arrived with a half bottle of white wine in it, and while the wine waiter opened it, our mussels arrived. When the waiters were gone, Dehan said, "You hear about the clam who joined the Ocean Gym to try and get a date?"

I sipped my wine. "No, Dehan, I never did."

"He pulled a mussel."

It made her laugh, and that made me laugh. After that, we ate in silence for a while, enjoying the food and the excellent, ice-cold wine. When we had finished, she sat back in her chair, wiped her lips with her napkin, and wagged a finger at me.

"You know what this reminds me of?"

"Nope."

"Peter Smith, Revere Avenue, two arms found in his lockup."[1]

I nodded slowly, thinking back to the second case we had worked together. "Jealousy . . ." I said absently.

"Different kind of jealousy, or maybe not. Somebody has something you haven't got."

"The dismembered body parts left in a place where they are sure to be found . . . There are parallels, that is true." I frowned. "As I recall . . ."

The wine waiter appeared by my side and poured me a drop of the red wine to taste, then, respectful of the new age of equality, he poured Dehan a drop too. We both sniffed and tasted, and he poured. Meanwhile the meat arrived, and we fell to with the kind of appetite you get from being by the sea. The meat was superb and so was the wine, and we got sidetracked into talking about all sorts of things that had nothing to do with Jack Connors' head, or the box it was in. But I didn't forget Dehan's observation, and it played on my mind all that night and into the next day.

We rounded off the meal with black coffee and Bushmills, and then a little more Bushmills, and finally left the dining room as they were switching off the lights and putting the chairs on the tables. By that time, Dehan was giggling at things that really were not funny, and I was smiling because I thought I was the luckiest man in the world.

I was.

––––––––

---

1. See *Two Bare Arms*.

THE NEXT MORNING, a cold shower followed by eggs, bacon, fried mushrooms, and lots of black coffee dispelled a small hangover, and by eight o'clock we were on our way back to New York, with Dehan looking up Shaw Line Defense on her phone. As we turned onto the I-95 and started to accelerate west, she sighed and shook her head.

"If we just turn up, they are going to stonewall us. I think we'll save time calling and making an appointment."

She dialed and put the phone to her ear. After a moment, she said, "Morning! This is Detective Carmen Dehan of the NYPD. I would like to make an appointment to see Mr. Grant Shaw . . . No, I don't want to tell you what it's about. That is something I will discuss with Mr. Shaw, when I see him. And believe me, I don't think he would appreciate my telling you either."

She went quiet, looked at me, sighed quietly, and raised her eyebrows. Then she listened attentively, sighed noisily, and said, "Ten thirty, we'll be there, and pal? If we need more than thirty minutes, he'll have to delay his damned flight. We're from the New York Police Department, we're not coming to measure him for a suit." She hung up. "Dickwad."

"I guess he knows who we are now."

"He can grant us—*grant*, note!—he can *grant* us thirty minutes at ten thirty and then he has a flight to catch."

"I gather you spoke to his secretary."

"Yeah. And I get the feeling the secretary is going to be pretty typical of the company."

I nodded. "I guess it goes with the territory. Arrogance."

At ten fifteen we pulled into 5th Avenue off West 23rd and parked just past the bus stop. I got out and looked up at the building. It was one of those attractive, gray stone, early-twentieth-century buildings, with discreet moldings on the outside and big, white sash windows. Penelope had been right, it didn't look like much, but to those in the know, to run that business in that location meant something. Dehan came and stood beside me.

"We're early."

I offered her a small shrug and we went in. The lobby was small and mainly white. There was a metal detector and beside it a young, athletic security guard all in blue. He inspected our badges and called up to the top floor. They must have told him it was okay, because he let us through and pointed us at the elevator.

The elevator was all shining steel and mirrors that concealed cameras and microphones. The only indication you had that it was moving at all was the changing number on the digital display, which went from one to seven in fifteen seconds, then stopped, and the doors slid silently open.

Reception was an almost featureless room, fifteen feet by twelve, without windows. Comfortable chairs on either side of the elevator faced a white desk that was made of a material that was hard to identify, but looked bulletproof. On the desk there was a logo, and the same logo appeared on the wall behind the desk. It was a circle bisected by a diagonal red line. The upper section was blue, and the lower section was white. I figured that was the Shaw line.

The receptionist was an expressionless blond guy who seemed to be constructed of pale granite. His hair was very short and almost white, and his eyes were a shade of blue you could use to halt global warming.

We showed him our badges and I said, "We're here to see Mr. Shaw."

"You're early."

"Yeah, we're early."

He took an electronic pad, like a tablet, and put it in front of us. "Can I have your thumbprints, please, then look at the laser for an iris scan."

Something about him, his boss, and his company made me feel irrationally uncooperative. I gently moved the tablet to one side and held my badge a few inches in front of his face.

"See this badge? This is all the ID that you need to see. Now we can do this in Mr. Shaw's office, or we can do it at an interrogation room at the Forty-Third Precinct. It's all the same to me. But as Mr. Shaw has a plane to catch, I suggest you tell him we're here and we would like to talk to him. Now."

He sized me up, and then he sized Dehan up, and he thought about kicking us out. I guess he decided it wasn't such a good idea, because he picked up the phone and after a moment said, "Sir, the cops are here early. They want to see you now." He waited a moment and said, "Yes, sir."

He hung up and pressed a button on his desk, then jerked his head at a featureless white door in the wall to my right. "Through there. At the end of the corridor. His secretary will let you in."

The door was steel and probably blast proof. I pulled it open and followed Dehan down a short passage to an antechamber with an oak desk in front of an oak door. Behind the desk was another Aryan clone with platinum hair you could sand rocks with. He looked at our badges without interest and said, "You're early."

"We covered that."

He curled a lip that said it was cops like us that were sending the country to the dogs and pressed a button on his desk. The oak door behind him buzzed and he jerked his head at it. "You can go in."

Clearly the big thing here was to have a button on your desk and jerk your head at the doors. Dehan sighed loudly and pushed through. The office was big, old-world, and luxurious, with oak-paneled walls, a burgundy Wilton carpet, Chesterfields, and an open fireplace that now stood cold. On the walls I saw two drawings by Matisse and a painting by Picasso. Grant Shaw was standing behind his desk putting things into an attaché case. He didn't look up as we came in. He just spoke loudly.

"We're on the clock, gentlemen. Make it snappy. We have ten minutes, then I am out of here. What can I do for you?"

I didn't answer him. We crossed the floor to his desk and got there as he was snapping his attaché case closed. Then he looked up and saw Dehan. The twitch of his eyebrows said he was surprised. I showed him my badge.

"This is the fourth time I've shown this badge since I stepped into your building. You're on the clock, Mr. Shaw, we are not. We are on a homicide investigation. I am Detective Stone; this is my partner, Detective Dehan, NYPD, and we need to ask you some questions. Is that a problem?"

He listened to me carefully, with no expression on his face. When I had finished, he said, "No problem at all. But I'd appreciate it if you make it quick."

"We haven't got time to waste either, Mr. Shaw. Can you tell us about your relationship with Penelope Peach?"

He laid his case down on the desk and stared at it for a moment. I moved around and sat in one of the two leather armchairs he had facing his desk. Dehan sat in the other, and after a moment Grant Shaw sat in his own big, black leather chair on the far side.

"Penny, what has she been up to?"

"Please don't answer my questions with questions of your own, Mr. Shaw, especially if you are in a hurry. We've all been around the block a few times, let's not waste time. Tell me about your relationship with her."

He shrugged. "What's to tell? I met her at some party, I think. She was a party girl. It's what she does for a living; at least it was back then. I'm going back about five years. We hit it off. She looked good, she was fun, so we went out for a while."

Dehan looked down at her hands, puffed out her cheeks, and blew.

"We have to do this, huh? We know. You know that we know. We know that you know that we know, but we still have to go through the bullshit." She looked up at his face. "We're not going to go away just because you bullshit us a bit, Mr. Shaw. Exactly the opposite is true. The more you bullshit us, the more we are going to keep coming at you, because here's the thing, bullshit and guilt smell just the same."

He went very still. "Guilt? Guilt of what?"

She gave an elaborate shrug and pulled the corners of her

mouth down. "I don't know. You're the one bullshitting, Mr. Shaw. What are you trying to hide?"

I shook my head. "See how much time we're wasting? And you in a hurry. How about we start again, you cut the bullshit, and maybe we won't even have to take you in. So, tell us about your relationship with Penelope Peach."

He sighed deeply and flopped back in his chair. "There really is very little to tell. I haven't seen her for a few years, but back then, four or five years ago, she . . ." He shrugged. "She made her living as a kept woman. That was what she did. And she was great. I really liked her. She already had an apartment that some joker was paying for, and she had a few other *friends*, that was what she called them, and me. So we started seeing quite a lot of each other, to the point where she actually phased out one or two of her other guys."

Dehan asked him, "So what are you saying? That you and she were getting serious?"

He thought about it, sat forward, put his hands flat on the attaché case, and drummed a tattoo with his fingers.

"Yuh. Obviously she kept on the guy who gave her the apartment, there was some other attorney I think who seems to have been pretty sweet on her, and there was me."

"So where was it going? What kind of future did a relationship like that have?"

He laughed, and his eyebrows both rose in a high arch. "Well, obviously none, because here we are."

I said, "But what did you want from it, Mr. Shaw?"

"You already know the answer to that."

"I'd like to hear it from you. Stop fencing with me."

"Fine! I had hoped for a wife. She suited me. She looked great, she had good taste and good manners, you could take her anywhere, people liked her. It would have suited both of us down to the ground."

I frowned, feeling suddenly curious. "But . . . ?"

"But she had suddenly got hormones or something, because

out of the blue she became all doe-eyed and romantic and went and fell in love with one of her Johns. Suddenly she was hopelessly in love and wanting to get married to him, not me."

I said, "To whom?" Dehan turned and frowned at me. She was thinking we knew who, Stephen.

Then her eyes opened wide as Grant said, "The guy, what was his name, who gave her the apartment. Jack, Jack Connors."

SIX

I HELD UP A HAND TO STOP HIM.

"Hang on a minute, Mr. Shaw. Let me just get this clear. Are you telling us that Penelope Peach told you that she was in love with Jack Connors and intended to marry him?"

The small frown told me he was surprised by the question. "Yuh, in retrospect it's not that surprising, really. He was the one who was willing to provide her with a luxury apartment on Riverside Drive, so I guess he got the prize." A small shrug, more from the eyebrows than his shoulders. "I was willing to give her a monthly allowance, but for real estate I expected something more."

I thought about it for a moment. "Did you ever meet him?"

He shook his head. "Nah, I'm not a jealous man, but I have my pride, and I don't care to socialize with the man who is fucking my girlfriend."

Dehan asked him, "How did you two break up?"

He looked up at the ceiling, slightly to his left. After a moment he said, "We went out to dinner. I can't remember where. I told her I wanted her to marry me. We'd discussed it a few times, but it had always been left in the air. Typical of a woman, she had a way of not saying no and not saying yes. It's like, the door is open but you can't come in—yet! So I had decided to press her."

"What happened?"

"She told me she was pretty serious about this Connors character. I forget what he did, might have been financial services . . ." He shook his head. "Something in the services industry, anyhow. She said she was falling in love with him and they planned to get married."

Dehan had a face like she'd just got five out of two plus two and didn't know how. She shook her head. "Wait, you are *sure* this is Jack Connors we're talking about, not some other guy, an attorney maybe?"

"Of course I'm sure. Aside from the fact that I have an excellent memory, it's not the kind of thing you forget."

I scratched my chin and asked him, "So, what happened after she told you that?"

He laughed. "We got drunk and had wild breakup sex in her apartment, in the bed bought for her by Mr. Connors. Lucky old Jack. That was typical Penny."

"You didn't row?"

He sighed noisily. "No, we didn't row, and I think, unless you're willing to tell me what this is all about, we are pretty much done."

I stared at him for a long moment, thinking it through. "You really don't know who Jack Connors was?"

He frowned. "Did I not make myself clear just now?"

I nodded. "You made yourself clear. Jack Connors was murdered the day after you broke up with Penelope Peach."

There was absolutely no change in his expression. He just nodded once and said, "You have to leave now. Any future communication will be through my attorneys. My secretary will give you their details."

I stood. Dehan leaned forward with her elbows on her knees. "Did you have Penelope followed?"

"Get out now or I will have you ejected. Out. *Now.*"

I gave him an empty smile. "Thank you for your time, Mr. Shaw."

We left.

Out on the sidewalk, Dehan turned and squinted at me in the late-morning sun. She fingered some strands of hair from her face and said, "What the hell was that about?"

I nodded as though I was agreeing with something she'd said and moved toward the car, turning the key over in my fingers. She followed after me. "Our prime suspect didn't even know who Jack was. He freaked out when he discovered he'd been murdered."

I unlocked the door and stood a moment, arranging all the people in my mind. She moved around the car and opened the passenger door. "Do you realize what this means, Stone?"

I frowned at her. "That he is even subtler than you thought?"

She stood motionless for a moment, then climbed in the car. I got in behind the wheel and closed the door.

She stared, first at the road ahead, then at me. "We'll explore that possibility in a minute. Right now, it looks to me as though he had no idea who Jack was or that he was even dead, let alone murdered."

I grunted and turned the key in the ignition. The engine growled, and I pulled out into the traffic, making for East 22nd and the FDR. "So what does it mean?"

"It means the subtle manipulator here is Penelope. It's what you said back at the hotel. The most convincing lies are the ones that are nine-tenths truth. It wasn't Stephen she was in love with, it was Jack. Like you said, if she was falling for Stephen, why did it take them almost five years to get engaged and married? The answer is, she was still carrying a torch for the man she'd loved and murdered."

I negotiated Park Avenue and turned right onto East 23rd, then began to cruise toward the river. Dehan was saying, "She fell in love with him and misread his signals. Shaw said it himself: he was the one willing to provide her with an apartment on Riverside Drive. So he got the prize. Penelope read that as a sign that he wanted to give her a home, that he was falling in love with her. She built up this whole fantasy in her head about how he felt the same way for her as she felt for him, and went so far as to break up with her billionaire boyfriend to be with him. Then reality comes crashing in and Jack tells her to forget it. He only wants her for sex. He's staying with his wife."

She stared at me while I chewed my lip. We came to the river, and I turned left and north and accelerated toward the Bronx. Dehan went on.

"So she kills him. And she thought she'd got away with it. Almost five years roll by and the case seems to be forgotten. She's moving on, getting married, making a new life as Mrs. Pillar of the Community. Only next thing we show up, digging up the past. So what does she do? She's subtle. She agrees to talk to us, but by careful phrasing she puts Shaw in the frame. He's the perfect fall guy. Killing people is his trade."

"Killing *is* his trade." I repeated her words. "You don't like him for it anymore?"

"When he said he wasn't jealous, I believed him. And he was definitely shocked when he realized why we were there. Plus, Stone, she lied to us! On two scores: she told us she was going to marry Stephen, not Jack, and, confusingly, she told us she *didn't* tell Shaw who she was planning to marry . . ."

"But implied that he stalked her with the white van . . ."

"So that we would conclude that he had had Jack killed."

I scratched my chin. It rasped. "We need to place her at the scene of the murder."

"We don't know where the scene of the murder was."

"That is exactly right. We also need to connect her with the weapon."

"And we don't know what the weapon was."

I nodded. "We are not even sure she had a motive. All we really know is that her story and Shaw's don't quite jibe."

She narrowed her eyes at me. "She's not getting to you, is she?"

I smiled. "Do I see your lovely brown eyes turning green, Carmen?"

"Don't be ridiculous. It's just guys can be really stupid when it comes to women like Penelope Peach."

I chuckled. "Girls can be just as blind when it comes to men like Grant Shaw. I think we've both been around the block often enough to be on our guard."

She frowned. "You still think he's a possible suspect?"

"I'm not sure yet, Dehan. I agree with you that Shaw is intelligent and subtle. When you say he freaked out, what I saw was a man in total control of his reactions. The conversation had reached a point where he no longer wanted to talk to us. So he shut down. His reaction could mean almost anything we wanted it to mean."

After a moment she grinned. "You thought I liked Grant Shaw?"

"Didn't you?"

"I thought he was a jerk."

"But an attractive jerk."

"He's got a kind of animal magnetism, but he's not my type, Sensei. You should know that."

"I do. We're straying a little off task here, Dehan . . ."

"I can't believe you were jealous . . ."

"I wasn't jealous. I just didn't think his reaction was as telling as you did."

"The great Sensei, jealous . . ."

I sighed, rolled my eyes, and settled to driving while she grinned at me from behind her aviators.

As we were pulling into the parking lot outside the station, my phone pinged to let me know I had an email. I read it as we crossed the road and made our way into the detectives' room. It was from Helena. I dropped into my chair and read it to Dehan.

"'Dear Detective Stone, blah blah . . . attached is a list of students whom I remember as having been in my class at the time of Jack's death. I cannot guarantee that it is complete. However, as far as I recall, these are the students I had at the time . . .'"

I printed two copies and handed one to Dehan, then dropped into my chair, staring at the page without seeing it. I started to say, "We may be losing sight . . ."

But Dehan interrupted me. "We have twelve names here. Two are girls." She looked up at me. "This feels like a male crime to me, but I agree with you that we should be open to the possibility that it was a woman. The rest are all guys . . ."

She sat, focused on the page, going through the names one by one. I wasn't thinking about the list, or the names; I was pretty sure none of them would mean much to me. Instead I was thinking about what had brought all those names together, on that sheet of paper.

Then Dehan looked up at me. "Dos Santos."

"Two saints?"

"Of the saints, it's Portuguese, not Spanish. Lenny dos Santos. I know that name."

"It does ring a bell. He's on the list?"

"Uh-huh . . . Fifty bucks says he's got a rap sheet."

While she checked, I looked through the list: Saul Adebayo, Julio Borregos, Zee Brown, Julian Calatrava, Susan Carter, Ernesto Cortez, Ira David, Mohamed Eze, Maria Garcia, Peter Heseltine, Lenny dos Santos, Toni Sotomayor.

There was a vague familiarity to several of the names. I thought aloud: "By the very nature of the classes, Dehan, more than one of these is going to have a rap sheet. That was the whole point of the exercise, after all."

She paid no attention to me. Instead she said, "You like apples?"

I looked up from the sheet. She was staring at the screen. She thumped the Enter key and said, "Well? Do you?"

"Sure, I'm not . . ."

She stood and walked over to the printer, came back with a couple of sheets of paper, and tossed one of them at me.

"Well, how'd ya like *them* apples?"

She read aloud as I scanned through it. She was the only person on Earth who could do that without annoying me.

"Leonard Arbuthnot dos Santos, twenty-nine years of age . . ." She shook her head. "This kid's been in and out of detention centers since he was thirteen: shoplifting, mugging, possession . . . Okay, he did time '98 to 2004, for assault with a deadly weapon. He was charged with attempted murder, but there was a self-defense angle and he pled to the lesser charge. Two years later he was charged with selling heroin but walked because the defense alleged the evidence was wrongfully obtained. He also beat a guy to within an inch of his life, but because it occurred concurrent with and as a part of the other offense, the evidence was also inadmissible. January 2015, he is arrested, charged, and successfully convicted for the murder of Mahalia Campbell, aka Cherry Cam, a prostitute. He was her pimp. She'd been skimming off the top to pay for her habit and he . . ." She looked up at me. "And I quote, severed her head with a kitchen knife."

"Oh . . ."

"Yes indeed."

"Them's powerful good apples, Dehan. Where is Mr. dos Santos now?"

"Upstate, in Malone, maximum security. He injured three cops during his arrest. He's a very bad man."

"Upstate? That's almost in Canada."

She was looking at her phone. "Yup, it's on the border. Interstate eighty-seven, five or six hours. Road trip."

"Does it seem strange to you that it never occurred to Helena to mention this guy?"

"Maybe she didn't know. He hadn't murdered anybody yet, and he'd been let off his previous offense on a technicality."

I sighed. "We'll see when we get there, but I am willing to bet he is not the shy, retiring type. I'm willing to bet he stands out in a crowd."

She flopped back in her chair and stuck a pencil in her mouth as though it were a cigarette. "She's just a crazy broad, Stone, with her head full of dumbass ideas about compassion and understanding, giving people a second chance, not judging people by their appearance. One of those New York liberals who never climbed out of her European car long enough to get mugged."

"You are a strange and disturbing creature, Dehan. Those are not dumbass ideas. I happen to believe in those ideas myself."

"Sure," she said with a deadpan face. "Me too. I was just kidding. When was the last time you were mugged, by the way?"

"I have never been mugged. But that has nothing to do with not getting out of my European . . . Call upstate, wiseass, make an appointment, and book us in somewhere comfortable. I'm going to call Helena and ask her about this guy."

"Sure thing, boss. Whatever you say, boss."

I called Helena. It rang twice, and a fruity, fluty voice said, "Aloh, Magnusson residence here. How may I help you?"

"Hello, Ebba, this is Detective Stone. May I speak to Mrs. Magnusson, please? It is quite important."

"Yoh, one moment please."

Fifteen seconds later, Helena came on the line. "Hello, Detective, I gather you received the list."

"Yes, there is one person on the list I am interested in. I wonder if you could tell me a little more about him."

"If I can, of course."

I glanced over at Dehan. She was talking into the phone and scrawling something on a piece of paper. I said, "Lenny dos Santos."

"Oh yes, Lenny." There was a smile in her voice. "He was amusing. We used to laugh a lot with Lenny."

"Really?"

"Yes, he was funny. Quite outrageous. I seem to remember he

was talented too. Of course no discipline, and no desire to understand grammar, or the mechanics of language."

"Sure, but I am more interested in what kind of relationship he developed with you."

"With me?" She sounded surprised.

I repressed a sigh. "Yes, of course. Did he admire you? Did he display affection toward you? Did he ever try to see you or talk to you alone, outside of class?"

There was a small laugh. "I have no idea if he admired me. He never spoke about my books, if that is what you mean. Displays of affection? He was big and noisy, and he was always embracing the girls in the class, me included, but not more than the others. I never saw him outside of class, Detective. If he ever made an attempt to see me, I was blind to it, or he was too subtle."

"Mrs. Magnusson, I need you to try a little harder. This is very important. Was there ever anything unusual, or that struck you as odd, in Lenny's attitude toward you?"

Again the laugh, with a faint patronizing whiff to it. "What have you done, Detective? You scanned the list and found the black student, and now he is your prime suspect? If you are suggesting that Lenny, or any of my students, was my husband's killer, I am afraid you are very much off track. Lenny was a kind, sweet, noisy clown who was incapable of hurting anybody."

"I see. I have just a couple more questions, Mrs. Magnusson, and then I'll let you get on. I notice here on the list Saul Adebayo and Mohamed Eze. Would I be correct in saying that they were both black?"

"Yes, Detective. Is that relevant?"

"Yes, Mrs. Magnusson, it is. Because neither of them is a suspect. The reason that neither of them is a suspect is that neither of them is doing time in a maximum-security prison for murdering a prostitute by cutting off her head. Lenny, on the other hand, is. He killed her, Mrs. Magnusson, because he was her pimp and she was stealing money from him to feed her heroin habit. Forgive me if I am a little brutal, but it seems to me that you need to face up to some facts and get real. Cuddly Lenny dos Santos had a rap sheet for violence going back to when he was a child. Now please, take that on board, assimilate it, and give it some serious thought. Then please contact me and let me know if anything in his behavior toward you was unusual."

She was very quiet. After a moment she said, "I see. I'm sorry. I will give it some thought."

"Thank you."

I hung up and looked across the desk at Dehan. She looked smug and had her pencil stuck in her mouth again. "Dumb broad, head full of crazy dreams."

"Cut it out."

"What did she say?"

"She wasn't aware of him behaving in any particular way. He was big and noisy and cuddly. He could probably have gone in there with a chain saw and she would have thought it was cute. What have you got?"

"Nine tomorrow morning. I booked us into the Kilburn Manor, in the heart of Malone. We're in the Judge's Suite."

Mo's voice intruded on us. "Course you did. Course you are."

I smiled over at him. Dehan stood and grabbed her jacket. "We better get moving, I also booked us a table at the Riverside Steak and Seafood restaurant. And it's a five-hour drive."

"Sounds good." I stood. "What are you doing tonight, Mo, anything nice?"

"Take a hike."

We stepped out into the midday sun.

SEVEN

MALONE SHOULD HAVE BEEN A NICE TOWN, AND pretty, but it was hard to escape the feeling, as we entered the town on Route 11 and drove onto Main Street, that we had slipped into a Stephen King novel. There was nothing you could put your finger on: the Mobil gas station was perfectly normal, and yet wore a strange air of desolation in the gathering dusk. The family restaurant looked cozy and friendly, but its roof looked strangely outsize and seemed to loom over the building. And as we approached the church tower, tall and very dark in the dying light, for a moment it looked to me like a vast, horned goat's head on a long, thin neck. And where the sky glowed a faint, dark blue through its arches, it looked to me like the goat's eyes.

"What is it about the northeast of this country that is so sinister at times?"

"You getting all freaky and weirded out, Stone?"

"Are you?"

"Nope. Cool-headed empirical realist, that's me. *Entia non sunt multiplicanda praeter necesitatem.*"

"Is that the only thing you can quote in Latin?"

"Yup, but it applies: don't let your imagination run away with you. It's probably just the presence of the maximum-security facility up the road, but you're right, there is a kind of eerie feel to this town."

I smiled at her. "Nothing a good, hearty meal and a bottle of wine can't take care of, huh?"

"You bet . . ."

But she didn't sound very convinced.

We passed the church, which was massive and made of dark gray stone, and turned left onto Clay Street, and at the end of Clay Street, half-concealed among trees, were the steep, gabled roof and portico of Kilburn Manor. We climbed out, grabbed our overnight bags from the trunk, and walked down the narrow path under the overarching shadows of the trees.

Kilburn Manor was in fact a B&B, but it was decorated and set up like a very luxurious old manor house. The manageress greeted us at the door and, as she led us up the stairs to our room, paused at practically every piece of furniture to tell us about its origins and its provenance. They were all antiques, she told us, including our vast, four-poster bed, which dated right back to the witch hunts.

We dumped our bags, showered, changed, and went out for dinner to the Riverside Steak and Seafood restaurant, which was just a short walk from the B&B. The walk confirmed the impression I had got from the car, that Malone was a strange and slightly desolate place.

On the way, Dehan linked her arm through mine as we walked.

"I think," she said, "that what has complicated things has been Penelope. I think she's like this charming whirlwind that goes storming through people's lives, and it's only after she's gone that they realize how much disruption she has caused."

"That's a nice image."

"And what we are seeing here is the evidence of where she passed through Jack, Helena, and Grant's lives, and because we are looking for evidence of a murderer, we *think* that is what we're seeing."

"Interesting."

"But, much like the case of the arms in the lockup, what we are actually seeing has nothing to do with the murder or the killer. The killer was elsewhere, observing the scene, and *his* interest was not Penny . . ."

"But Helena."

"Yup. Only in the lockup case, the killer had us seeing what he wanted us to see. In this case the killer is not that smart, he was just lucky. Penelope provided a kind of smoke screen, or at least a distraction."

We had come to a bridge on the long, strangely desolate Main Street, where ancient, cast-iron streetlamps with elaborate curls and twists stood in strange silhouette against their own dim, limpid light. We paused a moment, waiting for a gap in the sporadic traffic, and crossed to the far side, where the restaurant stood, spilling warm amber light onto the sidewalk.

We pushed inside into the warm. The lights were low, and the dark wood of the walls and the bar gave the place a certain gloom. A young waitress met us with a bright smile and showed us to our table near where a fire was burning in a grate. We sat, and I looked around. We needn't have booked. The place was largely empty, and, besides a murmur of conversation and some very quiet country music, it was almost silent.

We took the menus she offered us, Dehan ordered a beer, and I asked for a Martini, dry. I smiled and added, "It's not the same as a dry Martini, or a dry martini with a small *m*. It's two parts gin to one part Martini, over two large rocks, with an olive in it."

She smiled brightly and tilted her head on one side. "Sure. I can do that for you."

Dehan shook her head at the menu. "She didn't have to shake it instead of stirring it?"

"That's a Bradford and follows the *Savoy* recipe book from the 1930s. Whole different ball game. Tell me about how Lenny dos Santos is different from the killer in the lockup case."

"In that case, our guy deliberately manipulated the situation, actually stage-managed it. In this case I think it was almost accidental. Obviously we'll know more tomorrow after we talk to him, but the way I read it right now, he was a thug with delusions of grandeur. He heard there was a big shot novelist teaching creative writing in the neighborhood and decided he could do that. Maybe he had some notion about writing about his life of crime and cleaning up."

"Making a killing on a killing."

"Nice. Something like that."

I read from the menu: "Lightly breaded calamari, fried and served with a marinara sauce. That's me, or fried mozzarella, topped with mushrooms and roasted red peppers. That's you."

"Yeah, that's me."

"Then there are seven different kinds of steak. You can have it with cheese or shrimps or . . . you know." I made an "on and on" gesture with my hand. "Or you can have your twelve-ounce Angus rib eye with a choice of potatoes or French fries, the way it was meant to be."

"Yeah, that one."

"And draft beer."

"You done?"

I nodded and signaled the waitress. She came over with our drinks and I gave her our order. When she'd gone, Dehan sipped her beer and wiped her lip on the back of her hand.

"I think perhaps what we've been missing all along is something that you observed at the beginning, and then we got sidelined: that Helena was a fascinating woman." I nodded. She went on. "Fascinating enough, in fact, to hook a guy like Jack Connors and keep him from a woman like Penelope who must have been almost half her age. Dogs like Jack Connors need to sleep around or their ego pops and they die of emptiness when they realize how small and sad they really are."

"Wow."

"Way it is, dude. But he knew that Helena was something special and he hung on to her. Now, in spite of her naïve, simplistic view of bad guys, it took real balls to start that creative writing course in the heart of the Bronx. That in itself shows that she was something special, and she was a looker too, and five years younger."

"All true."

She took another pull on her beer and sat staring at it in her hand a moment, with a white foam moustache on her lip.

"I'm willing to bet," she said, "that every guy in that class had a crush on her, and maybe the girls did too. She was something special, something you don't see often. Now . . ."

"Along comes Lenny."

"Along comes Lenny. I'm going to do a Stone now."

I laughed. "Do a Stone?"

She wagged her finger at me, then wiped away her moustache. "I am going to extrapolate from known facts and reach a totally unjustified conclusion which happens to be right."

I laughed some more.

"From what we saw on Lenny's rap sheet, I am going to go out on a limb and say that this is one supremely arrogant son of a bitch who believes that he is entitled to everything. He's like Grant Shaw's extra-evil twin. Take what you want, and if they won't give it, shoot them and take it. He has decided that he is the dude and he can do anything, so now he is going to be a famous writer. He joins the class and within minutes becomes the class mascot. Everybody loves the dude, especially our naïve, idealistic, liberal do-gooder Helena. And the more she praises him as her special pupil, the more she feeds his ego and encourages him to believe that he really is the business.

"He's just a thug. I grew up with a hundred of them when I was a kid. He could be Irish, Puerto Rican, Mexican, or Nigerian. It makes no difference. He was an ignorant thug with an inflated ego. And she, in order to assuage her own liberal conscience, nurtured in him his totally unrealistic belief—A, in his own abilities and B, in the relationship that was developing between Helena and himself. How am I doing?"

"That is a lot of extrapolating going on there, Little Grasshopper, but it is also a pretty compelling story. Keep going."

"So, and here I am just guessing, but we're out for dinner shootin' the breeze, right? So I can guess. I am guessing that he began to send her messages. I don't mean folded bits of paper in his homework saying, 'I love you, Mrs. Magnusson, I want to marry you.' I mean messages in the stories he was writing, and in his banter. 'Helena and me, we understand each other. Am I right, Helena? You an' me, we got an understandin', right?' And she felt just like Everyman, or in her case Everywoman, or even better Everyperson, gathering up the lost to follow her to salvation. She thought she was transcending race, culture, and gender to help a poor, lost black kid; and *that* is irony right there, because what she was really doing was bringing her own middle-class white values and prejudices to a situation where they were woefully inadequate and inappropriate."

"Shall I ask the waitress for a soapbox?"

"Sorry. Anyhow, the point is there was a total lack of communication. He was telling her, 'You gonna be my bitch.' She understood, 'We have a deep, transcendent understanding and you are my guiding light.' She told him, 'I can lead you out of this hell you live in, to a better life,' and he understood, 'Yes, I am your bitch, and you are my man.'"

"I am troubled by the assumptions you are making, and also the stereotypes you are employing, but do go on."

"So, this miscommunication of intent . . ."

"Wait. Miscommunication of intent?"

"Yeah. He is telling her she is going to be his bitch. That is his intent. She is telling him she is going to save him. That's her intent."

"Okay . . ."

"This miscommunication reaches a climax of some sort. I don't know what, but clearly there comes a time when he wants to claim what is his. And she tells him he has got it wrong and she is in love with her husband. One way or another, that is conveyed to him. He is incensed, and in his rage he goes out, finds his rival, cuts off his head, and sends it to her."

I sipped my Martini, smacked my lips, and sighed. Then I nodded. "I know what you're saying, and in many ways I agree. But there are things that don't work for me. Like, for example, the guy you're describing. In my experience and in yours, he rapes her. He doesn't waste time on the husband. If he wants to make her, as you put it, his bitch, then that is what he goes right ahead and does. We're talking about a guy who decapitated a hooker because she was skimming off the top of his stash."

She pursed her lips like she was kissing the air and watched the waitress bring the calamari and the fried cheese. We put both plates in the middle of the table and shared.

With her mouth full of cheese, she wagged her fork at me.

"Okay, so let's not stereotype him. Maybe there were some self-fulfilling prophecies going on. Maybe he *did* idolize her. Maybe she was like no woman he had ever known. And his rage was directed against Jack. And after he killed him, before he could move on Helena, the classes were cancelled and he was arrested."

"Maybe. We'll see what he tells us tomorrow. One thing stands out, though. Whatever he was doing or saying, she was completely oblivious to it."

"Dumb broad."

I nodded and forked some calamari. "Naïve, certainly. So, Dehan, you figure Shaw and Penelope are out of the running now, and Helena herself."

She shook her head. "Nobody's out of the running, but I would say that Lenny is my prime suspect." Then she frowned. "He's not yours?"

I took some of her cheese and put it on a piece of bread. I chewed it, watching her across the table. "I'm going to wait till we've spoken to him. It's all speculation right now, Dehan. I'm having trouble with his choice of victim. I'm also having trouble with Shaw and Penelope. I can see them both as potentially capable of it, and yet . . ."

I watched her spear a calamari and stick it in her mouth, and added, "I am also very aware, Dehan, that we have not explored Helena as a potential suspect. That is a possibility we need to look at, and we also need to talk to . . ." I frowned, trying to remember his name.

She nodded. "Alornerk. It means clear sky or blue sky or something. The mathematician from Boston." She was quiet for a bit, putting cheese on her bread. "You seriously think she might have decapitated her husband? You think that's more likely than Lenny dos Santos?"

"We don't know, do we?"

"Okay, Sensei."

After that, we moved on from murder and decapitation to the increasingly familiar subjects of children and retirement. While we discussed these comfortable subjects, we worked our way through a couple of rib eye steaks, a couple more beers, and then a couple of whiskeys, and, by the time we stepped out into the strangely desolate Main Street, with its pallid yellow light and eerie, coiled streetlamps, and began our lonely walk back toward Kilburn Manor, the temperature had dropped to close to freezing, so that we could see our breath billowing before us and I had to tuck Dehan under my arm and my jacket to keep her warm.

We didn't talk then but walked huddled close against the cold, along the long, empty road, with its oddly ominous buildings, down Clay Street among the tall trees, to Kilburn Manor. There we found all the lights on, but nobody seemed to be at home. So we climbed the stairs in silence, among the ancient antiques and the loudly ticking clocks, to the Judge's Suite, where there was a fire burning in the grate.

EIGHT

LENNY DOS SANTOS WAS SIX FOOT SIX IN HIS BARE FEET. In his shoes he was almost six foot seven. He was big with it. Each leg was like a tree trunk, each foot easily fourteen inches long. His arms were the size of legs, and his chest, neck, and shoulders were like one massive slab of meat with his head perched on top.

The face on that head was a surprisingly cheerful, happy one. It was the kind of smiling face you'd expect to find on a garden gnome. As he was led through the steel door into the interrogation room, he regarded us with large, round eyes and smiled with an expressive mouth. The guard led him to the table and cuffed his wrists to a steel ring at the center.

"If he gives you any trouble, we're right outside."

We thanked him and he left. I said, "Hi, Lenny, I'm Detective John Stone of the NYPD, and this is my partner, Detective Carmen Dehan."

Lenny grinned at Dehan and then at me.

"Hi, it's nice to have visitors. Not many people come to see me. I ain't got family. Though my mom told me once I have cousins in Brazil, but I never met them. And my friends, well . . ." He laughed. "You can imagine my friends ain't real keen to come and see me in prison."

I nodded. "Sure."

His face became a little more serious. "But the truth is, I don't got a lot of friends, or maybe any, really. So it's nice to have visitors."

That thought made him smile again. Dehan sat back in her chair with a small frown on her brow, like she had decided to shelve all her questions and just study him for a bit. I offered him a smile that said I might be his friend and said, "Well, Lenny, you realize we're here on business."

"Oh, sure, I know that. They told me you wanted to ask me some questions. I don't got a problem with that."

"Thank you. You remember Helena?"

He repressed a smile and his eyes went wide. There was real amusement in his expression. "Man, I don't want to . . . I really don't like those guys who's always boastin', 'Oh, man! I been with so many women, I screwed this bitch and that bitch!' I hate that." He leaned forward, a look of delight on his face. "But I have to tell you the truth. A man like me, I was the man, you know? It ain't no exaggeration, couple of years or more maybe, I was with a different woman every night. Now, you do the math, that's like maybe a thousand women. I swear to you some of them I never knew and never saw again. Bro, it's like a blur. I ain't *proud* of that. I don't think that's a *good* thing, like some of these dudes in here. But you come to me now and you ask me, say, 'Do you remember Helena?' I gotta be honest with you. Just by the name, like that, I have *no* idea who Helena is. You gotta be more specific."

I studied his face, searching for signs that he was playing some wiseass game. I didn't find any. My impression was that he was being honest. I nodded.

"Sure, I understand. Do you remember at one time, about four and a half years ago, shortly before you were arrested, you had literary aspirations? You were doing a creative writing course."

"We got a group goin' here in the prison. I got some positive reviews in the prison magazine. 'Real, believable, and immediate.' I don't know what he meant by 'immediate,' but it was nice to read. You know?"

"Sure, I can imagine. Do you remember your teacher on that creative writing course? She was a famous novelist . . ."

His face lit up. "Oh, man! *Helena!* Well, sure! If you had just said, your writing teacher! Sure, I remember her. She was . . ." He smiled, shook his head, and gazed at the wall. "She was like . . ." He raised the fingers of his manacled hand. "Wait, I am going to try to express this. 'She was a ray of light in the darkness of my life.'"

He looked at Dehan to see what she thought of that. Then he looked at me.

"I think, if I had not been arrested, I would have left my life of crime anyway, just because of Helena. She made me see myself in a different way. She taught me, not just to be curious about *words*, but to have different expectations about myself." He leaned forward, his eyes wide with wonder. "If I use different words in my head, if I speak differently in my own mind, I can *be* different! That is magic, man!"

I nodded. "That's something."

He planted a big smile on the right side of his face and there was real humor in his eyes. "That's why they call it a spell. When you think that a letter is a symbol that makes a noise in your mind, you realize spelling is magic. She taught me that, man. She was somethin' special, I'll tell you."

Dehan spoke for the first time. "You a good student?"

"Sure, who wouldn't be with a teacher like that, right?"

"She punctual? Always there for class on time?"

"No, man, she was always there before class. She'd be there half an hour before class started, always."

"Yeah? That's nice, diligent. So, Lenny, how close did you and Helena get?"

He frowned at her, but without hostility. "I don't really

understand your question, Detective Dehan. Are you asking me if we was lovers?"

"Would you have liked to be?"

His face creased up and he started to laugh. It made him look like a fat, laughing Buddha.

"Oh! She was hot! No doubt! She was more than hot. She was *beautiful*! Inside and out. Any guy who got between the sheets with her was one lucky man. But she was strictly off-limits, know what I'm sayin'? She made that real clear." He laughed again. "I remember," he said, "somebody described a woman to me one time as having a sign nailed to her forehead that said, 'Fuck off. I'm married.' Helena was like that. Her husband must have been one lucky dude." He shook his head, still smiling. "She was way out of my league, man. Way out of my league."

He looked Dehan in the eye. "But, one day, Detective Dehan, if I ever get out of this shithole, if I ever make a success of writing, I would *aspire* to a woman like that."

She arched an eyebrow at him. "That is very inspiring, Lenny. So, you've told me how close you weren't. Now how about you tell me how close you *were*."

"We saw each other twice a week in class, Thursday and Friday. I was a pretty good student, so I didn't miss many classes. She was fun, she liked me. It was a nice class, we used to have a laugh. We'd all been around a bit, you know what I mean? We'd all lived some. We all had some stories to tell. First time in my life I didn't feel like I had to be a criminal. It was like . . ."

For a moment he seemed to be lost for words. I realized that was rare for him, and on impulse I said, "Coming home?"

He looked surprised and after a moment nodded. "Yeah, exactly. It was like coming home." He turned to Dehan. "You don't know this, but when you have no home, when you don't belong, you can be driven to do things you would not normally dream of doing."

Her face kind of stretched tight and she leaned back in her chair. I suppressed a smile and asked him, "Is that how you were driven to decapitate . . ." I paused, raising an eyebrow. "Do you remember her name?"

"Yeah, I remember her name. Cherry."

"Mahalia Campbell."

"We used to call her Cherry. You don't know. There are people in this world, walkin' among us, man, who are livin' in hell. There's some poet, I can't remember his name, he said, the mind is its own place." He turned to Dehan. "You know what that means? He says, it can make a hell of heaven, and a heaven of hell. That's fuckin' deep, man. When you belong, then it's like you're not in hell anymore. But when you don't belong, you can end up real fast in hell. And then you don't know what you can and can't do." He was still addressing Dehan. "I'll tell you somethin' else. When you don't belong, you know what the worst thing anybody can do to you is?"

She shrugged. "I know you're going to tell me."

"When you don't belong, the worst thing *anybody* can do to you is not kill you or cut you nor nothin' like that. It's steal from you. You're lost, you ain't got no home, nobody wants you and you don't belong nowhere, and then somebody steals from you. You gonna kill that motherfucker." He was silent for a moment, looking at his manacled hands. Then suddenly he said, "I'm sorry. I try not to talk like that. Helena taught me that the way we speak makes us who we are." He looked up at me. "I see a shrink in here, and he told me there is some truth in that."

"I'm sure there is. So you cut off Mahalia's head because she stole from you."

"Yeah. She stole my money . . ." He shrugged. "Though, in reality, if I could have seen things more clearly, it was her money because she was working for it. You know what I'm saying? But I was her pimp. I was crazy at that time."

"Did you feel that Helena belonged to you?"

He stared at me, with his eyebrows high on his forehead, then burst out laughing. "You crazy? Helena didn't belong to nobody! She was her own woman, man! What are you talking about?"

Dehan spoke suddenly. "Do you remember the last class, the one that was cancelled?"

"Yeah, we turned up and there was a sign. Said there had been an accident or some shit. Classes never started up again. But I knew she was okay 'cause she published a new book that same night. I read it. It was good."

"You ever meet her husband?"

The laughter faded from his face and he narrowed his eyes at her. "No, man. I never met her husband. What's this about, man? You ambushing me? Should I have a lawyer here with me?"

I shook my head. "We are not about to charge you with anything, Lenny. We are just trying to find out what happened that day."

"Well, why don't you *tell* me what happened that day?"

"You know that's not the way it works, Lenny. Can you remember what you did that Thursday?"

"That was five years ago. How the hell would I remember that, man?"

Dehan shrugged. "Maybe it was a notable day. Was it?"

"No. I don't know. I don't remember."

I said, "Does the name Jack Connors mean anything to you?"

He pulled down the corners of his mouth and raised his shoulders. "No. I don't know. Did I beat him up sometime? I beat up on a lot of guys. I used to be a real violent son of a bitch. I never lost a fight. You know that? Couple of guys I beat up almost died."

"I know. We've seen your sheet. Jack Connors was Helena's wife."

"Oh. She didn't take his name?" He smiled. "That's just like her. Independent woman." He stopped and frowned. "Wait. You said 'was.' He died and you want to pin it on me 'cause I was in her class? That's fucked up, man."

I shook my head. "We don't want to pin it on anybody, Lenny. We want to know who did it."

"Really?" He turned to Dehan. "Really? How many other people from the class you been to talk to?"

I answered. "None. We thought we'd start with you."

"No kidding. There was other black dudes in the class. Some were blacker than me. Why don't you start with them and work your way down to the white guy?"

"Believe it or not, Lenny, we didn't come to see you because you're black. We came to see you because you were the only person in the group who had decapitated somebody."

"What?"

"Jack Connors was decapitated. And that last class was cancelled because somebody sent his head to Helena in a parcel, to her class. Somebody who knew she had classes there on that day, and would be there half an hour before the class started."

His mouth sagged open. "Oh, man. That is fucked up. She was a sweet lady. I would not do that to her. She did not deserve that, man. No way."

"So what were you doing that day?"

"I have no idea. I can't remember what I was doing on that particular day five years ago. Nobody can remember somethin' like that. But I would not do that to her. She didn't deserve that."

I nodded. "Okay, so what were you driving at the time, Lenny?"

"Boy, you really out to frame me, huh?"

"No, Lenny. We are out to find the truth. And please remember that whatever you tell us, we will check and verify. If you didn't kill Jack Connors, that's good for you."

He sighed heavily, then smiled at the memory. "I had a bright red 1960 Cadillac convertible, red leather seats, drinks cabinet in the back, man, you never seen nothin' like that baby."

"You ever own a white van?"

"A white van?" He scowled at me. "Do I look like a fuckin 'lectrician to you? Or a fuckin' plumber? Car gives a man status. Car you choose says a lot about you. I always owned Caddies, since I was fourteen, when I bought my first wheels."

I drummed my fingers on the table for a moment, feeling there was something unasked and unanswered, but unsure what it was. I looked at Dehan. She shrugged.

"Okay, Lenny. That's all for now . . ."

He made a gun out of his manacled hand and pointed it at me. "You should look at the other people in the class, man. If they knew the time she would be there, half an hour early, either they was stalking her, or they were in the class. That class was a big mix of people, man. I can't remember them all, 'cause I wasn't real interested in them. But like I said, they all had a story to tell. And they all loved her. We all did."

Dehan narrowed her eyes and shook her head. "You'd send a decapitated head to the person you love?"

He looked momentarily mad. "No, Detective Dehan, I would not. But I can see how some people would, if they was in hell long enough; either to punish her for not loving them back, or as a sign that they had set her free."

I stared at him for a long moment, then called the guard. As the door rattled and clanged, I met Lenny's eye and said, "Thanks, Lenny. You've been very helpful."

And we left.

Down in the parking lot, a north wind had suddenly risen and was gently bowing the trees in the nearby woods. As we approached the car, Dehan turned and held out her hands. "Let me drive."

I threw her the keys. She snatched them from the air, unlocked the door, and turned to face me.

"Stone, what did you take away from that?"

"That he loved her and has no alibi."

"Seriously?"

"Uh-huh. Let's go surprise Alornerk."

"Boston?"

"I'll phone him on the way, see where he is."

NINE

ALORNERK WAS NOT PLEASED TO HEAR FROM US AND
questioned our authority to speak to him in Massachusetts when
we were New York cops. I told him it was an unofficial visit and
we were just trying to get a better understanding of the background to the case and what happened on the day of the murder.
He didn't like it but agreed to see us that afternoon at five. It was
going to be a five-hour drive from Malone, so that suited us fine.
For the first half hour, Dehan just drove and stared at the road
ahead, while I went over in my mind everything that Lenny had
told us. When I had gone over that a few times, I started going
over the case from every angle, trying to fit everything everybody
had said into a kind of 3D abstract puzzle.

I spoke my thoughts aloud and said to Dehan, "Let's look at
this from a different angle. Jack was taken and killed and decapitated in a very narrow window of time between one p.m. and five
p.m. on that Thursday. Allow for the head to be boxed and taken
to UPS and then delivered to the college and we are looking at a
window between one and four p.m., and that is generous. That is
a three-hour time frame in which the killer has to isolate Jack,
snatch him, take him to a location where he can decapitate him,
box up *and send* his head in time for it to reach Helena at college.

So, what are our pool of suspects doing in that period of time, between one and four p.m.?"

She sighed loudly through her nose. "Penelope says she was hungover, which means she had no alibi. Grant Shaw threw us out before we got the chance to ask for his alibi, but he confirmed the wild party with Penelope on Wednesday night, and in any case made it clear that if *he* killed anyone, he had plenty of pros to do the job for him. Helena was having lunch with Alornerk and his European friends, and he was having lunch with her and his European friends."

I scowled out at the passing trees in the exquisite springtime landscape. "So, so far the only people with alibis are Helena and Alornerk."

"And then," said Dehan with another sigh, "there are all the other people on her list of pupils *and*, if you want to feel really demoralized, all her fans."

I shook my head. "Unless we are dealing with a highly skilled stalker, I think we can discount her fans. This killer was familiar enough with Jack's movements to know that he was leaving for lunch, something, remember, he did not often do."

"That's true."

"Not only that, Dehan, he was able to kidnap him, drug him, and transport him to a quiet, secluded place in very little time, hardly leaving a trace of his—or her—presence."

"That takes a lot of skill, or at least detailed prior knowledge of his movements."

"So we are either looking at somebody with professional skills, such as a mercenary . . ."

"Yeah, you know, when you put it like that, it does kind of point pretty strongly to either Penelope or Shaw. Shaw has the kind of guys who could carry out an execution like that, and . . ." She stopped, turned to look at me, and shrugged. "Are we being a bit blind, Stone? I mean, where the hell was he going, if not to meet Penelope?"

I nodded. "And so far we have had no indication that he had any other lover at the time."

We sped over dappled shadows on the blacktop between tall walls of trees that towered over us on either side. She puffed out her cheeks and blew. "So, this suddenly looks pretty obvious, Stone. It's either A or B, right. I mean, A, she tells Jack Connors how she feels about him and that she wants to marry him. He blows her off. She freaks out, meets Shaw, lets off steam trying to forget Jack, but she can't—to the point where she actually tells Shaw she is going to marry Jack. Next day, she calls Jack and arranges to meet him to talk. He comes to her apartment, she drugs him, kills him, cuts off his head, parcels it up, and then disposes of the body. Feasible, motive and opportunity."

I nodded. "Yes, it's possible."

"B, she really was in love with him and he was in love with her. Shaw proposes and she says no. Remember his philosophy of life?"

"According to her."

"If you can't buy it, shoot the owner and take it. So his guy, in the white van, sees Jack arrive, and as he is leaving, he snatches him, bundles him in the van, yadda yadda." We continued in silence for a while along the dappled road and after a while she added, "They are the only two options that really jibe."

I frowned at her curiously.

"Why are you dismissing Lenny so easily?"

"I don't know."

"It is a hell of a coincidence, Dehan, and he just got through telling us he loved her and he has no alibi."

"Hmmm . . ." She glanced at me. "Is there any point in my asking what you think?"

"I think the narrow time frame is crucial. I think the familiarity with his movements is crucial. And the familiarity with Helena's schedule is crucial."

I smiled at her and was momentarily mesmerized by the

procession of trees moving across the lenses of her aviators. She said, "What?"

"There is one other person with a very powerful motive for killing Jack, perhaps the most powerful, who was familiar with his movements, knew about his affair, *and* was familiar with Helena's schedule."

She frowned. "Who?"

I raised my eyebrows. "Helena herself."

She shook her head. "Nah . . ."

"We need a lot more facts, Dehan. We should not write anybody off yet. You know . . ." I beat a tattoo on my knees with my hands. "You were right. This case does remind me of the lockup case. There are several things: the dismembered body, the fact that the rest of the body never showed, the fact that the head was delivered to a particular person in a particular place . . . all that, but especially the feeling that there is someone at the back of it all, watching and manipulating. That is the part that increasingly stands out for me."

She nodded for a bit and then shrugged. "That, for me, points to one of two people. Penelope and Shaw. They are both manipulators and controllers." She was quiet for a bit, then added, "Plus, Penelope was probably the last person to see him alive, if that is where he was going at lunch. That, Stone, *that* for me is crucial."

I thought about it and said, "I agree."

———

ALORNERK LIVED PRACTICALLY on the beach, on the corner of Quincy Shore Drive and Arnold Road. It was an ugly, two-story house with a gabled roof, a chimney, and an extension built over a large garage. The whole thing was set behind a chain-link fence in the middle of a flat lawn with no flowers.

I pulled into his driveway, blocking his garage, and stood looking out at Quincy Bay and the broad, sandy beach that led down to the sea. The front door of the house opened, beyond a dead flower bed, and a tall man with very long arms and legs stepped out and looked at us briefly. He was wearing black jeans and a black university sweatshirt, both of which made him look thinner. His pear-shaped head was balanced on top of his neck, so that the bulbous bit seemed about to overbalance at the top, while his chin barely protruded beyond his Adam's apple at the bottom. His hair was dark and short, and what little chin he had was unshaven.

He trotted down the steps to the lawn and approached us.

"Are you the detectives?"

"Detectives Stone and Dehan. As I said to you on the phone, we have no jurisdiction here. We are just hoping you can clarify . . ."

"Yeah, yeah, whatever. Let's go over to the beach. We can sit on the wall. I'm sick of being stuck in the fucking house all the time."

"Sure . . ."

But by the time I'd said it, he was already across his front yard, opening the gate and crossing the road. Dehan and I exchanged a glance and followed him.

Beyond the sidewalk there was a concrete wall, and beyond the wall there was a drop down to the white sand. Alornerk stood on the wall awhile, with the sea breeze whipping his sweatshirt, and as we crossed the road and joined him, he seemed to fold up and rearrange himself into a sitting position, looking out at the sea. Dehan sat on his left and I took my position on his right.

"I'm assuming you are Alornerk Smith?"

"Of course I am." He said it without inflection and without looking at me.

"We would like to ask you some questions about the day Jack Connors was killed. Have you any objection to that?"

"I assumed as much. Of course I have no objection. It was four and a half years ago, but my memory is pretty good."

Forty or fifty yards away, on the shore, a kid ran past, chasing a huge ball that was being blown by the breeze. It bounced and rolled in big bounds, and the kid's laughter came to us in ragged snatches.

"How is Helena?"

The question surprised me. "You haven't seen her recently?"

"Not in a while."

Dehan was watching the kid with his ball. He'd managed to catch it and was now running back toward his mother, holding it in front of him. She spoke absently, like she wasn't really interested. "You guys used to be pretty close."

"She used to work here, in the English Department. We became very close. Her husband was based in New York, she was based here. I thought it would go on like that forever. Then she had her first best seller." He looked down at his long, thin feet dangling from his long, thin legs. "It's almost unheard of, you know?"

Dehan asked the question. "What is?"

"For an academic in English literature to be a successful author."

"Oh."

"So I never really expected her to become a success."

I studied his face a moment. He still hadn't looked at either of us. "You were in love with her."

"When your whole life revolves around academic mathematics . . ."

He trailed off and looked at me for the first time. His eyes flicked around, examining every feature on my face.

"Because," he said, as though answering an unspoken question, "mathematics is everywhere, and everything, like God. It is the hidden meaning that inhabits all things. But in academia we take it and we abstract it so that all it has left is its numeric value. And then, when your whole life revolves around academic mathematics and numeric values, you can lose the ability to integrate abstract human feelings into your understanding of the world."

I looked back at the sea and saw that the little boy's mother had him now by his ankles and was holding him upside down.

The ball had escaped again and was being pursued into the sea by a red setter. "I can't imagine how you would do that," I said.

He shrugged. "Emotion is an entire chaos system in its own right. How can you give a value to a chaos system?"

"I wouldn't have thought you could."

"You can't."

Dehan looked up at the sky directly above us. The blue was an intense contrast to the white sand. "So, when you went to New York for the launch of her book, were you still lovers?"

He looked at his hands, at the palms; they were long and thin like his legs and his feet. Dehan sighed and added, "I mean, in the ordinary sense of the words."

Now he looked at her for the first time and nodded. "Yeah, I get bogged down in trying to understand the meaning of words and symbols, because there are no sharp lines separating one meaning from another . . ."

"Alornerk?"

He sighed and looked away. She persisted. "Were you lovers, in the ordinary sense of the word, when you went to her book launch in October 2014?"

He licked his lips and drew breath several times. "Yes, yes, we were lovers. Just, barely, anymore . . . How? How do you quantify dying love? And if you can't quantify it, how can you understand it?" He looked back at her for a moment. "Nothing hurts more than not understanding."

I nodded. "Not understanding definitely makes pain worse. No doubt about that. So, are you telling us that in October 2014, Helena had only recently moved to New York?"

"You didn't know that? Her first book had been a smash. And it was looking like the second one was going to be even bigger. Advance sales were off the chart. She told me she was moving to New York. She had some story about teaching creative writing to underprivileged people in the Bronx, but I knew the real reason was that she wanted to be closer to that Jack."

Dehan thrust out her bottom lip and gave a single nod. "That must have sucked."

He gave a small laugh. "You know about the styles of attachment? Bowlby? I am the anxious-ambivalent type. One of the characteristics of the anxious-ambivalent type is a highly acute sense of behavioral analysis. You can read people's behavior like it's a telegraphic message. I knew when she was lying, I knew when she was growing bored, I knew when she was preparing to leave me even before she did."

"Did you live together?"

"Not at first. I was married back then. But by the end of it, I was with her all the time. It cost me my marriage. For a while we were totally wrapped up in each other. It was very intense. We couldn't get enough of each other. It went on for months."

They hadn't noticed, but the big red, white, and blue ball had rolled out to sea and was slowly being carried away by the backwash from the waves. Mom was sitting on the sand, looking at her phone, and the kid was now chasing the dog instead of the ball.

I said, "And then her first book was accepted for publication."

"Yeah, and slowly everything began to change. I could sense it in the way she looked at me, the way she touched me . . . small changes in frequency and intensity . . ." He frowned at me with anxiety in his eyes. "Do you know what I mean? You can just tell that the smiles are less frequent, she spends less time with you because other things are becoming more important, she discusses her work with other people more often and more in depth than she does with you." He shrugged and looked down at the sand again. "You can see, you can read the signs, you know it is inevitable . . ."

Dehan said, "So, what? It was a year, eighteen months?"

"About eighteen months, and she told me she had made arrangements to spend more time in New York. Lots of excuses: her publisher was there, like that made any difference, she had switched to a New York agent her husband had found for her, she wanted to help underprivileged victims in the Bronx . . . A million and one apparently legitimate reasons, but at the root of it all was that her feelings for me were changing. Being with me was no longer important."

Dehan seemed to speak to his long, black sneakers. "This may be a painful question to answer, Alornerk, but it could be very important. Would you say that Helena and Jack were moving toward some kind of reconciliation? Were they growing closer again?"

He nodded for a while. "I don't know if it was a reconciliation exactly. They had a weird, fucked-up kind of codependent relationship. She was fucking me, he was fucking some other woman, but they needed each other. Is that love? I don't know."

We were silent for a moment, and as I drew breath to ask a question, he started speaking again. "She moved back to New York to be closer to him, to start living together again as husband and wife. The publication of her books was instrumental in that happening, and yet, on the day of the publication of her second novel, she was fucking me . . ."

I felt Dehan go very still. I looked out to sea. The ball was a tiny dot out on the ocean. I turned to look at him.

"Really?"

He nodded.

I said, "That isn't what you testified at the time."

"I realized that as I said it."

Dehan asked, "So where were your European friends while you were making the beast with two backs?"

He puffed out his cheeks. "There never were any European friends."

I gave a small laugh. "I'm sure you are aware we never really believed there were." He gave a small shrug, and Dehan gave a small frown to go with it. I ignored them both. "What you seem to be telling us, Alornerk, is that from about twelve midday to three or four o'clock, rather than having lunch at some unspecified restaurant with friends, you and Helena were having sexual intercourse."

I glanced at Dehan, who ignored me. Alornerk nodded. "She will be mad at me for telling you, but what have I got to lose now?"

"We'll come to that in a moment. First of all, I need you to tell me where this happened."

Dehan had her notebook out and was taking notes. Alornerk said, "In her house, in the guest room, because she didn't want to desecrate the sanctity of the matrimonial room. I should have . . ."

He stopped. I said, "What? What should you have done?"

"I should have walked out on her and gone back to Boston. Instead I believed that I could persuade her to leave that shallow, materialistic egomaniac."

I sighed. "Alornerk, what you are telling us is that the only alibi you have for the time of Jack's abduction and murder is Helena, with whom you were very much in love, and having an affair at the time of his death."

"I guess that is what I am telling you, yeah."

"Did you kill Jack Connors, Alornerk?"

"No. I was with Helena. We hadn't seen each other for some time. When we were alone together, she tried to resist, but the attraction was always too strong. He went to work in the morning. We finished breakfast, then went for a walk and talked things over. Next thing, we fell into bed and stayed there all morning. Eventually, after lunch, around three or four I suppose, she went off to her damned classes, and a couple of hours later, all hell broke loose."

Dehan studied his face for a moment.

"We will have to confront Helena with this, Alornerk, you realize that."

He shrugged. "I really don't give a damn anymore. Do your worst. She didn't kill him, and neither did I."

TEN

I SPENT A MOMENT THINKING THROUGH THE complexities of arresting him in Massachusetts as a New York cop and came to the conclusion it wasn't worth it, at least not yet. Instead I told him:

"I'm going to need you to come to New York to amend your statement. Are you willing to do that?"

"Are you going to arrest me for obstruction of justice or something?"

"I think we'd rather have you cooperate."

"You going to take me in now?"

"No. I need you to come of your own free will. But if you don't, we'll have to go down the whole extradition route and probably call in the U.S. Marshals, and you really don't want to go down that path, Alornerk. Right now you're probably going to get a smack on the wrist. But mess this up any further and then you'll find yourself in a real mess. I'll expect you at the Forty-Third no later than tomorrow afternoon."

He nodded. "Okay."

Dehan had been listening carefully, with a small frown. Now she said, "Before we wrap this up, I need to know if Helena was with you the whole time that Thursday morning, from the time Jack went to work until she left for her class in the Bronx?"

He thought about the answer for a long time, gazing out at the sea. I began to think he wasn't going to answer, but as I drew breath to prompt him, he suddenly sighed and said, "She was with me the whole time, yes."

"Why did you lie about going out to lunch with your European friends?"

He shrugged. "Because of this, what's happening now. It was her idea. I told her she should just tell the truth. Lying always leads to complications. But she said that if the cops did forensic tests on the bed and on us, and proved that we had had sexual intercourse, we would automatically become their prime suspects. Obviously Helena stood to inherit a huge amount of money from Jack, and as lovers we had a powerful motive . . ." He shrugged again. "So she said we needed to deflect their suspicion by concocting this story where there were other witnesses that we would try to track down. In the meantime, the investigation would follow its own course and they would forget about us. It was like one of her lurid novels. As it turned out, she was only half right. But she was very afraid of what would happen if the cops realized that we were lovers."

Dehan gave her head a small sideways twitch. "I got to tell you, it's not a good look, Alornerk."

He turned to gaze at her. "We were alone, but we were together, the whole morning up until she went to class."

I sighed and made to stand but paused. "There are two things you can do to really mess this up, Alornerk: go on the run, and call Helena to tell her what's happened. You understand me?"

"Yeah, I understand."

"So we'll see you tomorrow afternoon."

"Yeah, I'll be there early, about two or three."

I climbed to my feet and jumped down from the wall. Dehan swung her right leg over so she was straddling the wall, looking at him. She stopped there and said, "Whose idea was it that you should go to the book launch?"

"Hers."

"And hers that you should stay in the same house?"

"Yes."

"Did that strike you as odd?"

"No. She had gone back to him hoping that he would receive her with open arms. But she had forgotten what an asshole he was. He treated her like a worthless piece of shit, the same way he always had, and that depressed her. So I guess she had a whole mix of feelings and urges: to punish him in his own house, perhaps to make him jealous, to assuage her own feelings of inadequacy, to restore her self-esteem, all sorts of motivations for that decision to invite me there. None of them, I later realized, had anything at all to do with me, with making me happy, with making me feel good. It was all to protect and reinforce her bruised little ego."

"Yeah, I get that. Is there anything else you want to tell us before we go?"

"I didn't kill him, Detective Dehan, and neither did she."

"Okay, Alornerk, we'll see you tomorrow."

We left him sitting there, on the seawall, looking out at the breezy ocean as the sun began to slide down the dome of the sky toward the western horizon.

We crossed the road and made our way back to the car. On the way, Dehan tossed me the keys.

"Three and a half hours. Your turn."

We climbed in and I reversed out of the driveway onto Quincy Shore Drive and headed north in search of the I-90. As we crossed over the Neponset, she suddenly raised both hands and dropped them into her lap.

"We need some forensic evidence, Stone. We are just going round and round in circles. I . . ." She bit back the words, then sighed again and expostulated, "I don't honestly see how we can close this one, Stone! I mean, everyone might have done it, but nobody certainly did it . . ."

I made a skeptical face and said, "Not everyone might have done it."

She didn't hear me and went on. "I mean, our most likely person, like you said, is Lenny. Because, you know, he kills people, he cut off a woman's head, and he loved her and had no alibi!"

"I didn't actually say that . . ."

"But both Penelope and Shaw had motive and opportunity, and Alornerk and Helena lied about *their* alibi! Hell, Stone! We are no closer now than when we first picked up the case!"

"Possibly a slight exaggeration . . ."

"Do *you* believe Alornerk? Do *you* think he and Helena were in it together to get rid of Jack? She used Alornerk and then dumped him?"

"That's a novel theory."

"I mean, what the hell *do* you think, Stone?"

"I think you are right, we need some forensic evidence. I also think, as I did earlier today, that our very narrow window is crucial to what happened. Make a movie, Dehan."

"What?"

"Make a movie in your head."

"A movie?"

"It starts with Jack picking up the phone and arranging to meet Penelope. Maybe she calls him or maybe he calls her; we need to find out if the records were ever requested and, if not, whether they are still available."

"But wait a minute . . ."

"I know, Dehan, she said she didn't talk to him that day. But if she didn't, as I said before, who the hell was he going to see that lunchtime? So either he gets the call or he calls her, and he sets off to meet her. Either that or there is another person involved in this that we don't know about yet. Which I seriously doubt at this stage. So he sets off. What does he do? Does he get his car? Or does he walk? Whatever he does, in a very brief period of time he has been abducted. Now, Penelope's apartment is about . . ." I made a rapid calculation in my head. "Three miles from Jack's workplace. That's a ten- to twenty-minute drive. But he never makes it. He never gets there. So somewhere along that route, within ten minutes or so of his leaving his office, he has been abducted. That means that whoever took him was right there, waiting for him to go."

"That's true."

"But this is a very public place we are talking about, and nobody saw a struggle or a fight or anything of the sort. No witnesses were found who saw Jack being abducted, and we are talking about a strong man with a very aggressive personality. This is not a guy who is going to go quietly."

"So he knew who took him."

"Seems reasonable, doesn't it? Now, the rest of his task has to be performed rapidly and quietly and in time for the special delivery to be made punctually, in the Bronx."

She put her fingertips to her forehead. "So, so, so . . . wait! Penelope might have picked him up! Jesus, Stone! You're a genius! That's it! Of course! You said he would never go quietly, but he did because it was Penelope who picked him up. She *took him* to her apartment. The most natural thing in the world. Once there, she used ketamine to knock him out. Probably lured him into the bath where the mess could be easily cleaned up, dosed him with ketamine, killed him, cut off his head, and washed away all the blood, then parceled it up and sent the package. The message was, 'You want him? You can have him!' But how the hell do we prove it? How do we get forensics for that?"

I smiled at her. "We need the body. I doubt we'll find it, and after so long it's doubtful it would tell us much, but we should try and find it just in case. You never know. We also need that white van. That van is vital. Again, it's a long shot, but we may be able to piece together something from it. And finally the phone records from Penelope's phone, and Jack's and his company's phones. We need that call that made Jack leave his office. That is key."

She was silent for a bit, then said, "I get the call. The call is crucial, and the van. But I don't really see why the body is that important. I really don't see what the body could tell us after all this time."

I held up two fingers. "Two possible sources of information, Dehan. The first would be things like, was the body dumped whole—minus the head—or dismembered? That would help us to decide whether it was a man or a woman. A strong man might bundle the body in his trunk and dump it whole somewhere. A woman lacks the physical strength for that, so she might dismember it first and take it away in parcels. Also, if it was dismembered, can we identify what kind of tool was used? If it was whole, are there ligature marks? Were the hands tied? Or had he been, as you suggested, in a bath?"

"Okay, okay, yeah, I get it. What's the other thing?"

"Well, there is the outside chance that we are barking up the wrong tree and this was a motiveless murder."

"A *motiveless* murder . . . ?"

I nodded. "Is there more than one decapitated body out there?"

"*A serial killer?* What on Earth would make you think that?"

"You said it reminded you of the lockup. I get the same impression. What if the head was sent to Helena, not as a message to her in particular, but a message to the whole world? What if his obsession was not Helena herself, but married women and married men of a particular type? Are we finding this so hard because we are looking for a murder with a motive, where the only motive was to kill?"

"You really think that?"

"No, not really, but I think it is an avenue we need to explore."

"Because we haven't got enough to be looking into."

"We'll ask the inspector to give us some help looking for similar murders in the New York area during a year either side of Jack's murder. There can't be that many deaths by decap-itation."

"You have something on your mind you are not sharing with me. You know it makes me mad when you do that."

"Not at all. I am sharing with you everything that is on my mind. I am a reformed man, Dehan, you should know that: more caring, more sharing, more sensitive to my feminine side."

"You're a jerk."

"See, that's what I get for revealing my inner woman."

"Take a hike. Asshole." She smiled sidelong at me.

I said, "Dehan, please promise me something."

"What?"

"Never get in touch with your inner man."

"You done?"

"No. Especially if he has a big kind of Mexican moustache."

"Now are you done?"

"No. And hairy armpits. I think that could be damaging to the inner harmony of our inner relationship."

"Now?"

"Yeah."

"Is there anything you are not sharing with me besides your inner asshole?"

"No, seriously, Dehan. I don't think this is a serial killer, but I do think that we should cover that base and explore the possibility of other decapitated bodies."

"Why?"

I chuckled. "You mean what do I hope to find?"

"Yes, okay, the more closed question. What do you hope to find in such a search?"

I grinned at her. "Decapitated bodies."

"You are such a pain . . ."

"Do you mean, what would prompt me to search for further decapitated bodies?"

She didn't answer. She just stared out the window at the passing landscape. Neither of us spoke for about half an hour. Then she suddenly said, "Yes! Fine! That's what I meant! What would prompt you to search for further decapitated bodies?"

I offered her my most innocent face and shook my head. "I don't know. It's just a feeling. Call it a hunch." Then I sighed and shrugged. "There are a couple of things I don't get, Dehan. None of the suspects is quite satisfactory. There is always something that is not quite right. If Alornerk was so driven and so passionate about Helena that he was prepared to set up this elaborate murder, and not leave a trace, why the hell did he then give up on her without a fight? And the same goes for Lenny. It takes huge motivation to commit a murder like this. Yet, immediately after the killing, our murderer vanishes into thin air."

"Okay, I get that, but how does that lead you to more bodies?"

"It doesn't, exactly, but, to use your terminology, I have a feeling I can't shake of an observer. It may well be somebody we have already spoken to, one of our suspects, or somebody else. All I know is that this murder was put together in a very conscious way, and once it was done, the killer just seems to have vanished, walked away. That doesn't make sense. To my mind, the killer should either have made an attempt to take Helena for himself, or herself, or he should have killed again. So I want to look for . . ." I searched for the word. "I want to look for the killer's footprints, some evidence of their presence. It may be a wild goose chase, but it is one more thing we can do to try and find evidence of his or her presence."

She nodded. "Okay, I hear you, that does actually make sense."

"It's like, you know you read in books that somebody is walking along a dark road and they can feel somebody's eyes watching them. It's fanciful, stupid, but I can *feel* this person's presence, as though they are watching us conducting this investigation, and I keep going through our suspects, looking at each one, examining them in my mind, and each time I think, 'No, not him,' or 'No, not her,' I get this feeling that I have missed something."

"I never heard you talk like that before."

"Maybe you're rubbing off on me."

"You could do worse."

"No argument from me. I'd lay money though, Dehan, that the killer is right there, among our group, watching us."

"Don't forget we still have the list of other pupils, Stone. We have to go through them."

I nodded. "Yeah, yeah, I know."

ELEVEN

NEXT MORNING THE DEPUTY INSPECTOR AGREED TO give us a couple of officers to work methodically through murders reported in Massachusetts, Maine, Connecticut, and New York during the period 2014 to 2016, in which the victim was badly mutilated and in particular where decapitation was involved.

While they set to on their task, we got hold of the telephone records for Penelope, Connors Communication, and Grant Shaw, for the month of October 2014. As it turned out, we did not need to request them because the original investigating detective had already done that and they were in the file.

I sighed at the discovery and shook my head at Dehan. "When are you going to start thoroughly digesting the file *before* we start our investigation, Dehan?"

"When you start setting good examples for me, Sensei."

She made a second copy at the photocopier, dropped a wad of papers in front of me, and we set about examining them.

The first thing we looked for was the call Jack received on Thursday, October 7, at around one p.m. It wasn't there on his office phone, but it was there on his cell. It came through at twelve fifty. The only problem was, it wasn't Penelope's number. It was a number I was not familiar with.

I looked at Dehan across the desk. "He got the call on his cell at ten minutes before one, but it wasn't from her."

She nodded. "I'm looking at it, but go back a bit. This number calls him on a regular basis. The previous evening at six p.m. The previous morning at eleven and then again at one. The day before that it called him . . . one, two . . . four times. And the day before . . ." She leafed through several pages. "Every damn day."

I turned over a couple of pages to Sunday and Saturday. "Weekends too."

We stared at each other a moment. She said, "He can't have had two women going at that level of intensity . . ."

I was shaking my head, reading her thoughts. "But it's not two, because, where are her calls?"

I reached for her records and Dehan did the same. "Son of a gun."

I nodded. "It's her. She changed her damned number after he was killed."

Dehan was on her phone. I stood and went to look out the window, trying to think. I could hear Dehan's voice behind me. ". . . Detective Carmen Dehan, NYPD, I have an inquiry . . . No, it doesn't require a court order. I just need to know about a number . . ." She recited Penelope's current number. "It's registered to a Penelope Peach. I need to know when she acquired the number . . ." She waited a moment, then said, "Thanks," and hung up.

I turned to face her.

"Friday, October eighth. Whatever else she is, she ain't smart."

"You got that right. Listen, I'm going to talk to her. I want to know why she lied about calling him, what they talked about, and what happened after she called. I might bring her in . . ."

She was frowning at me. "Stone, this is very incriminating. We need to interrogate her."

"I know, but let me talk to her first, Dehan. Trust me, we are still missing something here."

Her eyes narrowed to slits. "And what am I doing while you're not interrogating Penelope Peach?"

"Look for the body—the bodies."

"That's stupid. I should go with you."

"Will you trust me? I'll be back in an hour and a half, two at the most."

She turned away. "Of course I trust you. I just think you're wrong."

"That's fine. I'll see you in a while."

I took a small detour to St. Lawrence Avenue before taking the Bronx River Parkway north to pick up the I-95 as far as the George Washington Bridge, before turning south, down along the Hudson as far as Penelope's apartment on Riverside Drive, opposite the tennis courts.

All the way, I was running Dehan's theory through my head. She would drive over first, be waiting for him, then call him, insist he comes down. He would get in the car, they would drive to her apartment. Then, according to Dehan's theory, she would induce him to get into the bath, no doubt with a bottle of champagne, and that was where it began to unravel.

There was, at every step of this case, something that was missing. The presence of ketamine in his blood confused me too. To be instantly effective, it would have to be applied with a hypodermic, and however hard I tried, I could not visualize the scene where the ketamine was applied that way. It just didn't ring true with Penelope or what I knew of Jack.

I parked on West 97th, made my way through the dappled shade to her apartment block, and showed the guy on the desk my badge.

"Is Ms. Peach at home?"

"Yes, Detective. She hasn't come down yet today. Shall I announce you?"

I shook my head. "No."

I rode the elevator to the ninth floor, examining the star-shaped patterns of inlaid wood on the floor, and myself in the mirror, wondering if I was getting my first gray hairs on my temples. The jury was still out when the elevator stopped and the doors slid back.

I stepped out into a red-carpeted passage that ran right to left, with brass lamps bolted to the walls. Two other passages branched off at right angles, one on my right and one on my left. Through them, sunlight made angular patterns on the floors and the walls. The apartment doors were walnut with walnut frames. I found her halfway down on the left and rang the bell.

There was a long silence. I was about to ring again when the door opened and Penelope stood staring up at me.

"John . . . What are you doing here? Where is Carmen?"

"Are you alone?"

"I . . ." She frowned. "Yes, I am. Why?"

"Can I come in?"

She paused, then nodded. "Of course." She stood back.

I stepped in and she closed the door. She smiled without feeling and touched her hair, which was uncombed. She was wearing a white satin robe. She should have looked stunning, but her skin was pale and pasty, and I wondered if she was hungover.

"I'm not long up," she said, as though answering a question I hadn't asked. "I'm making coffee. You want some?"

"Sure."

I followed her through a modern, comfortable living room to a bright, spacious kitchen with a breakfast bar. There she had a glass jug that was slowly filling with thin coffee from a filter. She took two cups from a cupboard. Her smile was nervous.

"Is this a social call? Should I go and put makeup on?"

"No. I'd prefer to see the real you."

"What's that supposed to mean?"

"It means I need you to stop lying." She filled a cup and handed it to me. I took it but I didn't drink from it. "My partner is mad at me. She thought we should just come and haul your ass into the station and charge you."

Her pallor became waxy. "Why?"

"That's what tends to happen when you lie to the cops, Penelope."

"What lie . . . ?"

I smiled. "You mean there is more than one?"

"No, I mean . . ." She shook her head. "I don't know what you're talking about."

"You know exactly what I'm talking about. And I'll go further. You have been involved in a pattern of deception since before Jack was killed. Now, my partner thinks that is powerful circumstantial evidence that you killed Jack. I think she may be right, but there are still things I don't understand. So you need to start persuading me that it wasn't you who killed him. You can do that by telling the truth."

"That's insane."

"Is it?" I sipped the coffee. It was weak and unsatisfying. "Why did you change your telephone number the day after he was killed?"

She closed her eyes, swore under her breath, and ran her fingers through her hair. She walked away from me. I followed her back through the living room and out onto a terrace over-looking the gardens along the river. She had a table out there and a couple of chairs. She put her cup there and sat. I put mine opposite.

"Don't start dreaming up more lies, Penelope. You're a bad liar, and the more you lie, the more you confirm our suspicions about you. You need to start coming clean and you need to start now."

"I was in a panic. I had just discovered that Jack was dead. Nobody knew about our affair, and I wanted to distance myself from him. I changed my number and my phone company and demanded that my old company destroy my phone records. They said they couldn't, but I kicked up a fuss and said I'd sue them, but I think they just humored me." She put her hands over her face and sighed noisily. "I just didn't want our affair to become public knowledge."

"Was that all? Penny, if you are putting two and two together, it must have dawned on you by now."

She turned to look at me and I could see she had not put two and two together and it had not dawned on her. I said:

"Your last phone call to him, Penny. You lied to us. You said you'd been out with Shaw, you were hungover, and you did not call Jack until the Friday. But that was another lie. You called him minutes before he disappeared. That is a very serious lie. You must see how that makes you look."

She dropped her hands into her lap and looked out over the rooftops. She had tears in her eyes. "You know I didn't kill him, John."

"No."

"But you said . . ."

"I said there were things I didn't understand."

"What? I'll explain anything you want. I'll do anything you want. I can't go to prison, John. I can't . . ."

"Stop. What did you call him for?"

"I . . ." She hesitated. "I wanted to talk to him about Stephen. He was taking it badly that . . ."

"You're lying. You really need to understand, Penelope. Every time you lie, you get one step closer to spending the rest of your life in prison."

"No!"

"If I ask Stephen when you met him, what is he going to tell me?"

She sat bolt upright. "No! You must not talk to Stephen."

"Wrong again. I agreed to keep him out of it as long as you cooperated. And all you have done so far is lie to me. Is that your idea of cooperation? Penelope, you don't seem to realize just how hard I can make life for you, or how close you are to being charged with murder. Now get smart and start cooperating with me, because I am the only thing right now standing between you and a murder charge."

"You're not serious . . ."

"Wake up, Penelope! You were the last person to speak to him! Minutes before he died! And you lied about it! Wake up!"

"Oh, Jesus . . ."

"What did you call him for?"

"We . . ." Her lips moved but she couldn't form the words.

"I spoke to Shaw. I know it wasn't Stephen you were planning to marry. He told me what you told him. You believed you were going to marry Jack."

She folded up, curled up into her own lap, with her face buried in her hands. She didn't sob or shake, but after a moment I realized she was crying.

"Did you kill him?"

"No, of course not!" She sat up, wiping her eyes with her sleeves. "I loved him. I *adored* him!"

"That's why people kill each other, Penelope." It came out with more bitterness than I intended. "Because they adore each other!"

"Don't be facetious. You have no idea how much I loved that man. It wasn't possessive ownership. I just worshipped the ground he trod on. He was . . ."

She ran out of words. She spread her hands, shrugged, and let them drop in her lap again. "He was a jerk, arrogant and obstinate. He knew it all and had all the answers. But nine-tenths of the time he was right, and when I had him alone with me, the barriers came down and the human being came out: funny, vulnerable, tender, *thoughtful*! My god, that man could be thoughtful. He was a bossy organizer, but driving that bossy organizer was a human being who wanted people to be happy."

"He was cheating on his wife and lying to her, Penny."

She stared me straight in the face. "Yeah, and that was wrong. But he was human, and fallible, and Jesus! You've met her. She is the cold fish to end all cold fish. She gave him nothing, and I gave him everything. He was happy when he was with me. He used to laugh. I have seen him on that couch in there, wiping his eyes, helpless with laughter. Nobody has seen that. He told me: with me, he learned to laugh. With me, he learned that there was more to life than achieving in business and making your workers happy."

"So why didn't he leave his wife?"

Again the direct, unwavering stare. "He did."

"*What?*"

"That's why I dumped Grant. You think I'd be stupid enough to leave Grant without knowing that Jack had left Helena? A couple of days earlier, he told me he had spoken to Helena, that they were finished and that they were going to discuss a divorce settlement that was fair and would cause minimal disruption. He said she had taken it very well—no great surprise there, right?"

I scowled at her. "And your reaction to this was to go and screw the boyfriend you were breaking up with? You sneer at Helena for keeping her cool, while you go and cheat on your future husband before you've even married him? You're mighty free with those rocks you keep hurling, Penelope, but I'd take care where you throw them."

Her cheeks flushed red and her eyes were bright, but she looked away and said, "I deserve that. But I'm afraid that was another lie. I asked Grant to lie for me and he agreed. He was very good about it. With him, it was only ever really the sex. When Jack was killed, he was good to me and agreed to give me an alibi."

"He didn't do a great job."

"I guess not."

"So now you're telling me you didn't have breakup sex."

"No, we didn't. We spoke, I explained we were finished and I was marrying Jack, and I went home. Then I called Jack and told him it was done, I had broken up with Grant. He said he'd meet me for lunch, and that was the last I ever heard from him."

"Where were you?"

"At home. When he never turned up, and it turned out he'd been killed, I panicked, put together an alibi with Grant, changed my phone, and just tried to put as much distance between us as possible. But I was devastated. It took me a long time to recover. I had never loved anyone the way I grew to love him. Never . . . never loved anyone like that since."

"So the white van was an invention too? A red herring to send the cops off chasing a ghost?"

She was already shaking her head before I had finished. "No, no, that was all true. I *did* have the feeling I was being watched, and I *did* see a white van a couple of times. That is absolutely true, and I will swear to that."

"Any reason I should believe you? All you've done since the first time we spoke to you is lie."

She didn't meet my eye this time. She just shook her head and said, "No, there is no reason you should believe me. But it's the truth."

"Who pays for this apartment now that Jack is dead?"

"He left it to me in his will."

"How did Helena feel about that?"

"I have no idea."

"You ever speak to her?"

"No."

"Can you tell me of anyone who would have a better motive than you to kill Jack Connors *in that particular way*, and send the head to Helena? Can you think of a single person who would have a better motive?"

"No, I can't." She looked out across the rooftops for a long moment, then swiveled her eyes to meet mine. "And that is why I panicked, and that is why I lied."

"I should arrest you, Penelope. I should take you in and charge you. Your story stinks and you look as guilty as hell. If my partner were here, she'd insist on it."

"Why don't you?"

I didn't answer. I sat for a long while looking at her, wondering what was stopping me. I didn't believe I had enough for an arrest, but at the same time I knew Dehan, and I should be dragging her over the coals and giving her a hard time, trying to find cracks in her story and force a confession.

I stood. "I need you to come in and make a statement, no later than tomorrow morning. At that time I will decide whether to charge you or not. You better pray that Grant confirms your story when I talk to him. Meantime, don't leave the city. If you try to, I will arrest you and you will be in deep, deep trouble."

"I'll come in this afternoon. John, everything I have told you is true. I lied because I panicked, but I am not a liar."

"There will be an officer watching your block. I'll expect to see you this afternoon. I'll see myself out."

I crossed the living room to the front door of the apartment, wondering at my own behavior and the motivation behind it. I opened the door and stepped out into the red-carpeted landing. The elevators were down on my left. A distorted lozenge of light lay across the carpet where it was beaming in from the passage on the left. I closed the door behind me and walked toward the elevators, still turning over Penelope's story in my head, and wondering what it was that had made me hold back from taking her in for interrogation.

I stopped in front of the elevator door and reached for the button.

That was when everything went black.

TWELVE

I OPENED MY EYES AND SAW ONLY BLACKNESS. I wondered for a second if I was blind but noticed patches of blackness that were less dark than others, where amorphous areas of density loomed and pressed in. There was panic inside me. I had no recollection of where I had been before the blackness, no knowledge of how I had got there. An impulse made me want to shout, call out for help. But my instincts made me hold back, lie still and quiet, and listen.

Then thoughts started to filter in.

Dehan.

She would be wondering where I was, which led me to wonder how long I had been wherever I was, and how I had got there. Where had I been before? What was the last thing in my mind, before the darkness?

Dehan.

Dehan had been mad at me. I could see her face, scowling. What had she been mad about? I hadn't been sharing my thoughts. That was what usually made her mad, but it hadn't been that. Not this time. She had been sharing her thoughts, about Jack's head, about Jack's murder, and the white van . . .

Penelope.

I tried to sit up and realized for the first time that my body was numb. A couple more attempts gave me pins and needles in my feet and my hands. And when I tried to reach my right hand with my left, it began to dawn on me that my wrists and my ankles were bound tight.

Then there was a moment when I felt real panic in my belly and fought hard with my mind to keep my thinking cool and rational.

Dehan.

I had told Dehan I would be a couple of hours. It must have been that long. I had been roughly half an hour getting to Penelope's apartment. We had been at least half an hour talking. Then what? Had I left? I struggled to bring back images. She had been crying. I had risen and moved toward the door. And then . . .

Then nothing.

If I had been clubbed or drugged, it would have taken at least half an hour to get me wherever I was, bind me, and leave me to come around. If Dehan was not already aware of my absence, she would be very soon. The only question was, soon enough?

I tried to concentrate on my sense of touch. Absurdly I closed my eyes, then concentrated my attention on my wrists. They were down beside my hips. I turned and twisted them and found they had a little give. They were bound with fine rope, not tape, and by the texture on my skin, it felt like nylon. There was not a hope in hell of breaking it.

I tried to sit up again, slowly, and found there were a couple of ropes across my chest and shoulders. I was pretty much immobilized, and even if I were able to move enough to reach my pockets, I had to assume my cell had been taken. There was an outside chance my GPS was on and traceable, but it was unlikely, to say the least. It dawned on me that I must be going through something very similar to what Jack Connors went through during his last hours, but it was poor consolation.

I spent the next while—it could have been half an hour or ten minutes, it was impossible to tell in that darkness—just listening. I heard nothing: no traffic, no voices, no birds, no foghorns. Nothing but my own breathing.

The surface I was lying on felt like wood, and as I explored what little area I could with my fingers, I realized I must be lying on a table. The surface and the edges were not smooth, like a polished dining table, but slightly rough, so I began a slow and hopeless process of rubbing the ropes binding my wrists against the edge of the table in the hope of wearing through them. Though it seemed more likely the rope would wear through the wood.

After a long while, I heard a noise. It might have been a bump, or a footfall. I froze. After a moment, there was the clack of a key turning in a lock and a thin strip of light broke the darkness. How near or how far it was was impossible to tell, nor did the light reveal anything of where I was, or what lay beyond it. It was just a strip of brilliance in the dark. Nothing happened for a moment. Then the brilliance expanded and at its center there was the black, spidery silhouette of a person standing with one hand outstretched, pushing open the door.

I waited. The figure was hazy and seemed to shift, perhaps take a step closer. I squinted, but I couldn't make out any detail. I spoke, and my voice sounded strange and loud.

"Who are you?"

There was no indication they had heard, or even knew I was there. I spoke louder. "Come and untie me!"

The figure remained motionless, its right hand raised, outstretched against the blackness of the door.

"The whole of the NYPD will be searching for me. They know where I went. You can't get away with this." Still nothing, no reaction, no indication it had heard. "Let's talk! Let's negotiate! Tell me what you want."

Again nothing. I flopped back, rested my head against the

tabletop, and closed my eyes for a moment, trying to think. When I raised it again to look, the figure had come almost imperceptibly closer and was now filling more of the doorframe, with the brilliance behind it. Now I could sense that it was staring at me. Panic coiled like a snake in my belly. I said, "Is it Helena? Is that what you want?"

Nothing shifted, nothing changed, except that I could sense the intensity of the figure's concentration.

"Why didn't you kill her, instead? Why kill Jack? Which one of them was it who hurt you? Or was it both? You have a story. I'd like to hear it. I am not out to punish anyone. I am just out to understand."

I knew I was overreaching and stopped. The figure seemed to recede slightly. I spoke again, more quietly. "So it was Helena. She was at the heart of the whole thing, wasn't she? That's why it wasn't enough to kill him. That's why you had to send her the head."

The shadow receded a little more and the door started to close. I shouted: "Did she appreciate it?"

The door stopped. I shouted again: "*Did she appreciate what you did?*"

The blackness contracted around the jagged hook of light and shut it out. There was a clack, and the blackness was locked in.

———

DEHAN HAD WATCHED me leave and sat for a while thinking about dismembered bodies and decapitation. Finally, she had called Frank at the morgue. She had said:

"We're averaging three hundred murders a year just in the city, double that in the state."

"What's your point, you're being forced to do your job?"

"Hey, save the attitude for Stone. I'm the pretty one. You're supposed to be nice to me."

"So what do you want from me? I'm the guy who has to deal with those three hundred murders. I am actually trying to *do* my job. And, FYI, it's below three hundred now."

"Quit griping, Frank. All I want you to do is think a little. This is the kind of body that is going to stand out from the rest. He hasn't been mangled or chopped up with a machete. His head has been cleanly severed in one swipe, with something like a samurai . . ."

"I am familiar with the decapitation, Carmen. It was I who described it to you, if you remember."

"If there had been anything similar in 2013, 2014, or 2015, surely it would have stuck in your memory; a body with the head missing, or some kind of dismemberment where the limbs had been removed with surgical precision . . ."

"What crackpot idea is Stone playing with now? He thinks this is a serial killer?"

"He thinks it's worth exploring, and I kind of agree. It is a very odd way to kill somebody."

"Yes. Not as much as you might think, but yes. However, the startling feature is the mailing of the head, not the severing of it." He sighed, then muttered, "There was something. But it wasn't New York. You realize this city has processed around one thousand five hundred homicides since 2013 . . ."

"Yeah, well, that's kind of why I'm calling you, Frank."

"I simply haven't got the time to go looking for it, but I can point you in the right direction. It stood out because it was in Connecticut, where, as you know, the locals don't kill each other. I read about it in the *Journal,* it was in one of those coast towns that are so pretty, New Haven, Guilford . . ."

"Madison?"

". . . yes. Yes, I believe it *was* Madison."

"What was it? What was the homicide?"

"Please bear in mind that I only read about it in our professional journal. This was not my jurisdiction. *As I recall,* it was a male body, midforties, well dressed, not in the system so back then he had not been identified, and he had been decapitated. I *believe* it was a single, clean cut. The article was actually about the state of decomposition when the body is exposed to the elements in extreme cold. The article was in the spring issue so, if memory serves, the body was found at some point during the winter, 2014 to 2015."

Dehan frowned and scratched her head. "Well, could it have been Jack Connors' body?"

"Of course not, Carmen. John Doe's DNA is in the system. We searched for matches for Connors and none popped up."

"Sure . . ."

"That really is all I can do for you, Carmen."

"Yeah, thanks, Frank. That was really helpful."

She hung up and immediately called me. It rang a few times and went to voicemail.

"Stone, something has come up you really need to know about. Your hunch paid off, and this could be a lot more complicated than you think. Call me as soon as you get this."

She found the case report and spent the next hour trawling through 2013 homicide reports where there was some kind of mutilation involved. She found nothing of any interest. Shortly before lunch, she called me again and got my voicemail again. That made her nervous because it was totally out of character for me not to answer her calls.

At that point, Consuelo, one of the team who had been assigned to review the homicides from 2013 to 2015, approached her desk.

"You got something?"

"I think so. We found this report filed by the Fairfield County Sheriff's Department." She handed her the extract from the file. "White male, midforties, found in Sherwood Mill Pond, Westport. That's just past Norwalk, like thirty miles from New Rochdale?"

"I know where it is. I drove past it just the other day."

"The body had been decapitated and dumped in the pond.

The cut was described by the ME as having been made with surgical precision. It was found April 2015. I called the Fairfield Sheriff's Department and they said the body has not been identified or claimed, and the head was never found."

"That's excellent work, Consuelo. Thanks, keep digging. But do something for me, will you? I want you, personally, to focus only on 2013 and 2014. Forget 2015."

"Forget 2015?"

"Yes."

She nodded. "Okay, sure, I'll do that."

After that, she made her way up the stairs to the chief's office. On the way, she called my number again and again got my voicemail. She went upstairs and knocked on the deputy inspector's door.

"Come!"

She stepped in and he smiled at her. "Carmen, what can I do for you?"

She took a moment to organize her thoughts, then outlined the case.

The deputy inspector listened and nodded. "I remember it. It caused quite a stir at the time."

"Yes, sir. It was always assumed, and we assumed, that the murder was about Jack Connors and Helena Magnusson."

He frowned. "Logically, it would be."

"But, as you know, Stone had this notion we should look for other similar bodies . . ."

The deputy inspector made a face of long suffering and sighed. "Yes, how's that going?"

"Well, sir, as always, it's beginning to look as though he was right. But it gets more complicated." He gestured at a seat, and she sat across the desk from him, still talking. "Jack Connors had a lover, Penelope Peach. We discovered that, contrary to what was originally thought, Penelope believed that Jack was going to leave his wife and marry her. Penelope had lied about this in the original investigation, and later to us."

"I see . . . Carmen, where is John?"

"That's the thing, sir. She didn't only lie about that. She also claimed she hadn't spoken to Jack on the day he died, but in actual fact, she telephoned him shortly before he left the office and was never seen again. Stone went to confront her with these facts."

"Oh."

"But there is more, sir."

"More?"

"While he was talking to Penelope, I was helping the team to look for prior cases of decapitation. We have found two. Now, here is where it gets a little complicated, and I don't really know what it means."

"Spit it out, Carmen."

"We first met Penelope in Madison, Connecticut. She said she was visiting her fiancé's senior partner. So, to avoid awkward questions, we met her at the hotel. Now, as I said, we have discovered two bodies, both from 2015, both decapitated with surgical precision, one in Madison and the other in Westport, forty miles from Madison, roughly halfway between here and there, and on the same highway."

"Have you discussed this with John? What does he say? Where is he?"

"He is not answering his phone, sir. I've called him three times so far and it just goes to voicemail. It's been . . ." She glanced at her watch. "It's been a little over two hours."

"Take a couple of cars and go to her apartment. Bring her in. Why didn't he do that to start with? Why didn't he bring her in straightaway?"

She sighed. "I don't know, sir. When he's on a roll, he doesn't always share his thoughts."

"He should have brought her in, and you should have insisted, Carmen. We'll talk about this after. Right now, get to her apartment, bring her in for interrogation, and find John. And as soon as you get back, I want you both in my office, before you interrogate her. I want to know what the hell is going on, I want to know what is in John's mind, and I want to know why we have three decapitated bodies. I mean, what the hell! Have we got a serial killer, or what?"

"Yes, sir."

"Why are you still here? Go!"

THIRTEEN

I OPENED MY EYES AND REALIZED I HAD BEEN ASLEEP. I still felt groggy, and the light was hurting my eyes. I tried to shield them with my hand but couldn't move it and remembered my hands were tied. Then the memories started to seep back. My belly burned and I felt sick. It had been dark. Now it was light. Somebody had switched the lights on.

I opened my eyes by slow degrees and peered. A wave of intense nausea washed over me and for a moment I thought I was going to vomit, but it passed, and I tried to take in what I was seeing. My vision was foggy, and at first it didn't make a lot of sense. I had a strange sense of dissociation, as though I were watching myself, understanding myself and my relationship to the universe for the first time.

On my left there was a bare brick wall. It felt cold on the back of my hand. I muttered to myself, "There is cold, but I am not cold." I raised my head and looked down the length of a body that was mine, but not me. Thin nylon rope bit into my throat, but I could see my shoes, and beyond them a jumble of boxes, old chairs, a standard lamp—junk. No windows.

I smiled, aware that what I was seeing was a symbol of my past, which was holding me prisoner.

Then I turned to my right. More cartons full of junk, photographs in frames, an old computer, wires, keyboards. Some concrete steps; I counted them: six, leading to a door. The door that had opened and then closed, where the shadow had stood. I wondered if the shadow had been me, observing myself. There was no source of natural light in the room. No way of measuring time. Everything was now. I stared up at the ceiling: the dirty, white wire protruding from the bare concrete, the ancient green glass shade, the forty-watt bulb.

I craned my neck against the thin nylon rope across my throat and tried to see the floor. It too was concrete, dusty, littered with bits of card, scraps of paper, and amorphous trash that was impossible to identify.

I flopped back and looked to my right again. That was when I slowly became aware of the bench that was just a foot or two from my head and just above the height of my shoulder. It looked like a workbench of the sort you might have in your garage, for sawing wood or doing odd DIY jobs. But it was slightly different, as though it had been modified in some way. It had a system of rollers and pulleys I could not quite make out, but as I narrowed my eyes and tried to focus, I realized that, fed through the rollers and pulleys, there was a thin steel wire, like a piano wire.

Or a cheese cutter.

And it was threaded up and over my throat. What was holding my head down was not just a nylon rope; there was a thin steel wire too.

With that realization came the realization also that I was on the clock, and a confusing feeling that I was already dead. Time was running out. While I had been sleeping under the effects of whatever drug I was being given, my captor had been in there with me, preparing me for decapitation. I was running out of time, and I was running out fast. I tested my ligatures again and realized that if I tried to force the wire around my neck, it would slice into my flesh. I had to release my hands first, but I had no idea how. I looked down at my right wrist and saw where my attempts to fray the rope earlier had bitten into the table but had done nothing to the rope. My head was reeling. My stomach was panicking, and my dissociated mind was embracing death.

The sound of the key in the lock made me look over at the steps. The tumblers clunked and the door swung open, but where earlier the light had been on outside, now it was off, and all I could see was the darkness of a corridor in shadows, and within it, the slightly darker shadow of a person's silhouette, standing motionless, watching me.

I watched it back for a while, wondering again whether I was lying on the table or standing in the shadows, watching myself. A long time seemed to pass, but it may have been just twenty or thirty seconds. Finally I said, "Is that all we're going to do, stand there and stare?"

Nothing happened. There was no response. The figure remained motionless, watching me. The words spilled from my mouth as though of their own accord.

"What do you think you are going to achieve by killing me? I am you and you are me. We are one. Life is death and death is life. It's all the same. Besides, this place is going to be swarming with cops within the hour, like an anthill. Nothing changes because I die."

Then I heard something. It was like a sniff, or a slight hiss. It dawned on me that it was a snigger. A feeling of sinking dread seemed to drain me from inside. "You're out of your mind," I said, but the words sounded suddenly hollow. I realized that he was lost *inside* his mind, and I was out of mine, and free. "It's not too late. Cut me loose and stop this before you get completely lost. I can show you the way back."

There was movement, a shuffling of feet, and the figure seemed to grow within the doorframe. I strained my eyes to make out some detail. I imagined I could see some pallor where the face was, but hard as I strained, the details fogged and merged and became hazy.

I flopped my head back again. "You must realize that you are in a maze. You must realize that you are in a game of Troy. The only way out is death. You can't kill me, I am already disembodied. But you, you are lost."

I looked again. The shape shifted, warped slightly, and the door slowly closed.

———

DEHAN TOOK AN UNMARKED CHARGER AND, with two patrol cars, headed with sirens howling along the Cross Bronx Expressway and, at the George Washington Bridge, hurtled south down the Henry Hudson Parkway.

They screeched to a halt outside Penelope's block and Dehan scrambled from her vehicle shouting to Vazquez and Torres, "*Stay on the door! Get security! Find out if there is a rear door. Cover every damn exit on the building!*"

And as they ran to their task, she bellowed at Günther and Brown, "*You! With me!*" and stormed into the lobby, holding her badge in front of her. The guy on the desk looked startled. Dehan snapped at him, "Detective Dehan, NYPD. Get security! Has Detective Stone been here?"

"Yes, Detective. He went up, oh, two hours ago? A little more . . . Ninth floor, Miss Peach . . ."

"Just the two elevators?"

"Yes!"

"You two." She pointed to Günther and Brown. "Take that one. I'll take the other." To the guy on the desk, she snapped, "You, get security to cover the stairs. Nobody leaves!"

They rode to the ninth floor, and as the doors slid open, she pushed through and ran down the red-carpeted passage to the walnut door where she hammered with her fist, bellowing, "*NYPD! Open the door! This is Detective Carmen Dehan! Open the damned door!*"

As Günther and Brown caught up with her, she drew her

piece and they drew theirs. She hammered again and rang the bell. "*NYPD! Open up or I'll kick down the door!*"

The door opened, and Penelope stood staring at her. Her face was pale, and her hair was drawn back from her face. She was still in her satin housecoat.

"Carmen . . . Detective Dehan, what on Earth?"

"Is Detective Stone here?"

"He was, a couple of hours ago, but he left. What is this about?"

"Ma'am, we have cause to believe that a serious crime might have been committed in this apartment, and we are going to enter and make a search. Please stand aside."

"*What?*"

One look at Dehan's face told her not to argue, and she stepped aside. Dehan pushed her way in, snarling over her shoulder, "Every room, every wardrobe, every cupboard. Search the damn toilet cisterns! I want every nook and cranny in this apartment scoured!"

When they had disappeared into the bedroom, Dehan turned on Penelope, took a handful of her satin gown in her left fist, and rammed her against the wall. When she spoke, her voice was an ugly rasp.

"Between you and me, sister. You like taking other women's husbands? You like hurting them? Let me put you on notice, babe. If you have touched him, if you have breathed on him too hard, I will make sure not a day goes by for the rest of your miserable life that you don't weep and regret what you did today. Do we understand each other?" Before Penelope could answer, Dehan pushed her face closer, so they were barely an inch apart, and whispered, "Let's cut the crap. I promise you, if you have hurt him, the law will not protect you. He's my partner, but he's my husband too, and I am a bad, *bad* bitch from the Bronx."

She held her eye for a long moment, then let her go and said, "Now, Penelope, is there anything you want to tell me?"

Penelope stared at her wide-eyed. "You're out of your mind."

"Count on it. Where is he?"

"He was here, but he left."

Günther and Brown came out of the bedroom. Brown made for the kitchen, and Günther went out onto the terrace. Dehan repeated, "Where is he? What have you done with him?"

Penelope's voice began to rise. "I keep telling you, he was here, and he left!"

Günther's voice came from the terrace. "Detective, two cups of coffee out here!"

"You'd better start talking, Penelope. You'd better tell me where my partner is or things are going to get real ugly for you."

Her voice was getting shrill. "Will you please *listen* to me! He came here. He had found discrepancies in my story. He wanted to know why I had changed my telephone number, why I had lied about calling Jack . . ."

"I'm pretty curious about that myself."

"We talked and I explained it. When I had finished, he said he wanted me to go to your station house this afternoon and make a new statement. I was just getting ready to go when you showed up. He left, and that was the last I saw of him."

"You called Jack and lied about it. He came to your apartment and disappeared. Stone catches you in that lie, comes to your apartment, and disappears . . . You'd better pray he turns up safe, Penelope. You'd better pray. Get dressed, you're coming down to the station."

Penelope gave a ragged sigh and went to the bedroom. Dehan gave Brown a nod and she went with her.

"Günther, go down. You, Vazquez, and Torres start canvassing the area, start with security and the guy on the desk, I want to know who saw Detective Stone leave and where he went. I want to know who he was with. Also, search the area for a burgundy Jaguar Mark II, 1964, right-hand drive, with spoke wheels. It shouldn't be hard to spot. Put a BOLO out on the car and on Detective Stone. Somebody saw him leave. I need that person. Go!"

Penelope emerged from the bedroom, dressed and with an overnight bag. Dehan told Brown to join the search and took Penelope down in the elevator. In the lobby, she met Torres coming in.

"Detective, we found Detective Stone's car."

"Where? Where is it?"

He looked embarrassed and a little confused and gestured toward the street. "It was right outside, less than a block down the street."

Dehan stared at Penelope. Penelope looked scared. Dehan grabbed her and shoved her at Torres. "Put her in my car. If she tries to run, restrain her. Use any necessary force. I'll be right out."

Torres led Penelope out to the cars, and Dehan went to the desk, where the guy on reception and the security guard watched her approach with the kind of expression you usually reserve for an important guest who's just thrown up at your dinner party. She said to them:

"Think, and think hard. The life of a police officer is on the line here. You saw Detective Stone arrive and go up to Ms. Peach's apartment."

"Yes."

"She swears he left, but his car is parked outside. Did you or did you not see him leave."

The porter shook his head, and his expression was adamant. "I have been on the desk all morning, I did not see Detective Stone leave after he went up to Ms. Peach's apartment."

"Back exit? Service entrance? Some other way out?"

The security guard shook his head. "No, no. Nothing of that sort."

She hesitated a moment. "Then Ms. Peach has some other property in this block. She must own or have access to another property?"

The porter looked startled. "No, not at all!"

Dehan's voice was rising. "A parking garage, a storeroom!"

"No!"

"Goddamn it! Detective Stone did not just vanish into thin air!"

The man drew himself up with dignity. "That is as it may be, but Ms. Peach *still* has no other property here!"

She scowled at him, and then an idea began to form in her head. She pulled her cell from her pocket and called the inspector.

"Carmen! What news? Was he there?"

"No, sir. So far it looks like he left and stepped into the Bermuda Triangle. He has vanished without a trace, but his car is parked just outside. The doorman swears he did not leave. I have checked, and Penelope Peach does not own any other properties in the apartment block, or have access to any of them."

"Then where in God's name . . . ?"

"Sir, we need to know who owns the other apartments. We need to know if Grant Shaw owns any of them."

"Good heavens! What are you . . . ?"

"It stands to reason, sir, if he didn't leave, he's here. If he isn't in her apartment, he's in somebody else's apartment. It's a process of elimination. Who else might have an apartment in the same block as her? Not Helena, not Lenny dos Santos . . . but maybe the man she was having an affair with."

"All right, yes. Good thinking."

"I'm going to take Penelope in, sir, she's in the car. I'm going to start grilling her . . ."

"I'll make inquiries about the other apartments. Meanwhile, canvass the area in case anyone saw him leave."

"Already on it, sir."

"Good. I'll send more men down, with photographs. He'll turn up, Carmen."

"I know, sir. Thank you."

She went out and found Torres standing by the unmarked Charger.

"I'm taking the suspect to the Forty-Third. You have more men coming, with photographs. I want everyone, *everyone*, canvassed in a four-block radius. Check the block too, apartment by apartment, show them the photograph. Somebody must have seen him."

"If he's here, we'll find him, Detective."

Torres left to join the search, and Dehan climbed in the car. She fired up the engine and pulled out into the traffic, heading back toward the Bronx. She studied Penelope's face in the mirror. She looked scared. Dehan spoke, keeping one eye on her reflection, watching her reactions.

"We're checking the property register to see who owns the other apartments in your block."

She saw Penelope frown. "What?"

"If Stone didn't leave, he is still in the block, in one of the apartments. If not yours, then somebody else's."

Penelope shook her head, frowning harder. "Well, who do you expect to find on the property register?"

"What do you think? Who do you think we'll find?"

"I have no idea, Detective. I honestly have no idea what happened to him after he left."

Dehan curled her lip. "Sure, only your honesty ain't carrying a lot of weight at the moment, Penny, and I have a funny notion we are going to find Grant Shaw on the property register, or at the very least Shaw Line Defense. What do you think?"

She didn't answer for a moment. She just stared at the back of Dehan's head. Then she said, "What does that mean? What are you driving at?"

Dehan raised an eyebrow at her reflection. "Let's save it for the interrogation room, but it's beginning to look to me like your relationship with Grant Shaw might have gone a little bit beyond the bedroom, Penny. And that is an idea I am increasingly keen to explore."

Penny closed her eyes and sagged back against the seat.

FOURTEEN

The door opened, and this time the lights were on in the room and also in the passage outside. The figure in the doorway was clear now: black high heels, black stockings, a black dress to just above the knee, blond hair tied back, and a black lace veil over her face. The figure was familiar. I struggled to focus, but my sight and my mind were still foggy and I sagged back.

Rage and frustration welled inside me, but I fought them down. Rage would not help me now. My body was incapacitated. The only weapons I had were my mind and dialogue. I had to start a dialogue.

"Thank you for letting me see you."

The figure took a couple of steps and came into the room, standing at the top of the steps. I kept talking.

"I didn't recognize you at first. You were always in the shadows, but I had a hunch it was you."

It might have been my imagination, I still felt oddly dissociated, but for a moment I had the sense that the words had struck home. Vanity wanted to be satisfied. How had I guessed? I smiled.

"It was a process of elimination. There were mistakes you made . . ." I made a show of hesitating. "Don't get me wrong. If I hadn't come along, you'd probably have got away with it. But I am pretty good at this, and the people you were pointing at . . ."

I left the words hanging and shook my head.

The figure turned and descended the steps, disappeared momentarily from view, then loomed over me, looking down into my face through the black veil. The image was grotesque: tragic, infantile, and terrifying. The voice, when it came, was, like the face, twisted and distorted with pain and hatred.

"I made no mistakes."

"Come on! Lenny? Way too obvious. And right from the start, the first thing I thought about Lenny was, 'He decapitates women, not men!' And then only in a rage. No, he had no beef with . . ."

Again I left the words hanging and struggled to focus on the tortured face behind the black veil. The red lips moved. "Jack."

"Did you love him?" There was no reply. I pressed on. "Or did you hate him? Or was it both?"

"You are not here to understand. You are here to set me free."

The long, delicate fingers reached out to test the tension of the wire across my throat. I spoke quickly, trying not to sound desperate, and failing.

"Then why the mourning dress? Isn't that a message? Aren't you trying to tell me something? Who's it for if not me? Who else is going to see it?"

The pale eyes stared at me for a long moment, then whispered, "*Me, me, me.*"

The figure turned away and walked around the trestle bench where the wire was connected to the pulleys. I saw the delicate hand reach down and take hold of a white, plastic handle to which the wire was attached. There was an urgency in my voice that was bordering on panic.

"Whatever you did, right? Whatever you did, it was never enough. However much you shone, it was never enough; never enough to catch his eye and make him stop and notice! You were invisible! You could have left him. You could have left him a hundred times. But you kept coming back to him. But he never really *saw* you."

A sad smile. A smile that had given up asking for compassion and was now willing to turn away and allow the most brutal cruelty. The fingers closed on the banal plastic handle. One pull, I knew, would pull the wire with horrific force through my throat, slicing cleanly through tissue and bone.

"Tell your story! A jury might understand. It would not be the first time a man like that had been killed for his arrogance and his cruelty. If you can secure a sympathetic jury . . ."

"You know nothing of my story. Like everyone else, all you see is him."

"I am trying to see *you*. I am trying to hear you. Tell it. Tell your story! You have the skill, haven't you? Isn't that what you do?"

"You are patronizing me."

"No, I am showing you how to walk away from the biggest mistake of your life. You are a wordsmith. You can weave magic with words. Make people understand how destructive a man like Jack can be. Make them understand how he destroyed lives, how you had no choice in what you did."

"You don't know what you are talking about."

"How do you know that? Do *you* know *me*? What *do* you know about me? Jack I can understand. You knew him intimately! But me? You know *nothing* about me. And yet you are willing to destroy me. For what?"

"You don't know anything about my relationship with Jack. Nobody knows anything about my relationship with Jack."

"You keep saying that, but the way to make me understand, the way to make everyone understand, is not this. It's *words*! Tell your story. The world will be fascinated."

"It is too late for that. I tried to do it. It didn't work. You only know half the story, Detective Stone."

"Tell me the rest. Help me to understand."

"Stop."

I drew breath, closed my eyes. I didn't want to show fear, but I could hear my breath shaking. The voice in my ears was quiet, reasonable, relentless.

"It is time to die now. Make peace."

"I know you were in love!"

"Past tense?"

"I know you still are. But I know you were not in love with Jack! I know you grew to hate Jack. I know that the other love was —is—all consuming! I know you would do anything for that other love! I know it drove you to kill, and not just once. There have been others, haven't there? And now you feel you are trapped in hell, inside your own mind, and there is no way out and no redemption for you. I know that, and I know other things too. I *do* understand and I *can* help you to find a way back, but you have to *talk* to me. You have to tell your story!"

"You are wasting time. Make peace, Detective Stone."

"It is not me who needs to make peace! I am already at peace. It's you! You are the one who turned love into a motive for killing. You are the one who started and couldn't stop! You are the one who opened the doors to hell! You are the one being sucked in, out of control! You are the one who needs to make peace, not me!"

"Stop saying that."

"Step back before it is too late. Release me. Cut the bonds and take the wire from my throat. It is not too late to make this right. Do it now and I promise you, I *promise* you I will help you find redemption. The judge, the jury, they will show leniency."

Again the sad smile. "You are a brave man, a warrior. I admire your spirit. You don't give up. But you are out of time. Make peace. The time to die is now."

I saw her hand move. I felt the sharp pain, and then there was nothing.

———

Dehan and Deputy Inspector Newman stood outside the observation booth for interview room three. Newman was not happy, and neither was Dehan.

"You should not be conducting this investigation, Carmen. He is not only your partner, he's your husband. Your objectivity is compromised."

"With all due respect, sir. My objectivity is not the issue here. The issue is finding Stone, and nobody in this precinct can do that better than I can."

"I want you to partner up with . . ."

"Sorry, Chief. That is not going to happen."

"Excuse me?"

"Priority one: find Stone. I do *not* need to be worrying about a new partner or whether I am being objective. I need to be interrogating my witness."

"Carmen."

"Sir, do you know *why* I was partnered with Stone?"

"Carmen."

"We were partnered because there wasn't a detective in the Forty-Third who would work with me because I had such a bad attitude, and Captain Cuevas wanted to *punish* Stone by partnering him with me."

"*Carmen . . .*"

"Sir, I do not need to be worrying about hurting the feelings of some pussy-assed, chauvinistic dickhead when what I *do* need to be doing is finding Stone! I'm sorry! I won't do it!"

"*Carmen!*"

"*What?*"

"*Shut up!* Good Lord, woman! Go and find Stone!"

"Thank you, sir."

With that, she turned and pushed into the interrogation room.

Penelope was sitting at the table, looking pale and strained. Her eyes followed Dehan as she crossed the room and sat across the table from her.

"Okay, Penny, I am going to try and make this fast and easy for you. Where is Stone?"

"I don't know. I told you already. I. Don't. Know."

"Fact: he went to your apartment. Fact: he was in your apartment. Fact: he has disappeared. Fact: he has not been seen since he arrived at your apartment. Fact: his car is still parked where he left it when he went to your apartment, and fact: nobody saw him leave your apartment or your apartment block. Now, you tell me what a jury is going to make of those facts. You tell me what, as a detective, I am supposed to make of those facts."

A spasm of irritation tightened Penelope's face. "There is a fact you are missing, Detective Dehan! The *fact* that he was not *at* my apartment when you arrived and *must* therefore have left!"

"Which leads us to the inescapable conclusion that he is still in that apartment block. So where have you got him? Where did you put him, Penelope?"

"I didn't put him anywhere. I don't *know* where he is!"

"Who are you working with?"

"*What?*"

"Who took Stone from your apartment?"

"Are you out of your mind?"

"Come on, Penelope! Cut the crap! We have cops crawling over that building like ants! You think we won't find him? Do you know what will happen to you when we do find him?"

"You are out of your mind! Why in the name of God would I abduct Detective Stone? What possible reason . . ."

"What date have you set for your wedding, Penelope?"

"What? Why . . . ?"

"Stephen, isn't it?"

"Yes, but threatening me won't do you any good, because I don't . . ."

"Rich? Successful? Great prospects, right?"

"Yes, but . . ."

"So, just going out on a limb here, Penny, but I'm guessing that facing trial for the murder of Jack Connors would have been pretty damaging for your prospects of marrying a big shot Manhattan lawyer."

"Of course it would! But I am not crazy enough to kill a damned police officer because of it! I am not insane! And who the *hell* do you think my accomplice is? Mrs. Brown upstairs? She's eighty-four next June! Or perhaps the Epsteins next door?"

"Or perhaps it's Grant Shaw."

"This again? Okay, so we stayed friends. I lied about us falling out. But it was exactly because of this *bullshit*! I *knew* that you would do this! I have not got a thing with Grant! We broke up years ago. We have barely stayed in touch. The son of a bitch couldn't even keep his story straight when he spoke to you. You think if he was my 'accomplice'"—she made speech marks in the air with her fingers—"he would have told you I was going to marry Jack? No. He would have told you the *same goddamn story I told you*!"

"Does he own a property in that block?"

"No!" She did a kind of double take. "No, you know what? *I don't know!* Maybe he does? I don't know what he owns in New York! Maybe he owns the whole goddamn block for all I know! Maybe he owns the whole fucking island!"

"We'll know very soon."

"Good! Maybe then you can give me a goddamn break! I have not abducted your partner! I am not that stupid! And I do not have an accomplice in some diabolical plot to abduct New York cops!"

"What time did he arrive?"

"Again?"

"What time did he arrive?"

"I told you. I don't know the exact time. It was about . . ." She sighed. "It was about three hours ago, maybe more."

"What did you talk about?"

"I *told* you already! He wanted to know why I'd lied. He wanted to know why I changed my phone. I *told* you already! Do I need a lawyer?"

"It's up to you. You're engaged to a big shot, call him."

Her face said that wasn't an option, and she covered her eyes with her hands, then ran her fingers through her hair. "I want to cooperate, but you are making it so hard, Carmen."

"Where is Stone?"

"*I don't know!*"

There was a knock at the door, and a uniform poked his head in. "Detective, the chief wants to see you."

"Okay, I'll be right there." The uniform left, and Dehan turned back to Penny. "I'll be back. Meantime, you'd better do some serious thinking, Penny, because your story does not wash. I am going to keep coming at you, and I will not stop until you tell me where Stone is." She leaned forward across the table. "And if you have hurt him . . ."

She left the sentence unfinished, stood, and stepped out into the passage. The deputy inspector met her outside the door.

"Just heard. Look, Carmen, I'm sorry, none of the apartments belong to Grant Shaw. There are a number of private owners, a couple of banks, investment companies. I've emailed you the list. But none of them are traceable to Shaw. Besides which, the officers have drawn a blank. They've gone over the building from the roof to the cellar. The neighbors were all cooperative and helpful. They have found nothing. It's a dead end."

She stared at him for a long moment, then shook her head. "It doesn't make sense. He has got to be in that building. He didn't leave. Nobody saw him leave. His car was still there."

"He is not there, Carmen. Focus. John does not need a wife right now. What John needs is the best damn detective at the Forty-Third. Now focus! If he is not there, where is he?"

She rubbed her face with her hands, took a deep breath, stared at the wall, then the ceiling, then at the inspector.

"Okay. Baby steps: he is not there, so he is somewhere else. Nobody saw him leave, so he left without being seen. Right?"

"Right."

"So we need to be looking at people that left the building

during that period, during that window, but were either not seen or not recognized. Stone left, or somebody left with Stone, during those two hours, and somebody saw him, without realizing what they were seeing. Right?"

"Exactly!"

"Security cameras!"

"Good! Go and get it."

She turned and pushed back into the interrogation room. She went to the table and leaned across, looking deep into Penelope's eyes. "I need to know exactly what time Stone left your apartment."

"I don't know exactly . . ."

"He left here about ten, half an hour to get to you, maybe forty minutes to reach your apartment. How long were you talking?"

"Not long, maybe twenty minutes or half an hour."

Dehan turned and bellowed, "*Sergeant!*" A sergeant poked her head around the door. "Take Ms. Peach to a holding cell."

She pushed out of the room again and made her way to the inspector's door. She pushed in without knocking and he looked up at her.

"Sir, the security camera footage from eleven a.m. and for the next hour. We need the elevator and the lobby. And hell! Anything else they have. But if he left the building, he will show up on that footage."

"I'll call. You go. But Carmen . . ."

"I know, sir. We are looking for someone . . . or something . . . that does not look like Stone . . . I know."

FIFTEEN

SHE DROVE FAST, BACK ALONG THE ROUTE SHE HAD taken earlier in the unmarked Dodge Charger with the siren howling to the fading afternoon. She screeched to a halt outside Penelope's block and ran into the lobby. The porter was waiting for her with the security guard and led her to a small room in back, behind the desk. As they went, Dehan was talking to the security guard.

"I want the ninth floor. I want the landing, I want the elevator, and I want the lobby, ten minutes to eleven o'clock through to twelve noon. Everyone who comes out of the block. One of those people who comes out is my partner."

"Yes, ma'am. We don't have cameras on the landings. But when your inspector called, I started going through . . ."

The porter interjected, "I told you your partner never came out, Detective."

"That's the truth, ma'am, there ain't no sign of him. I have the photograph your boys brought around earlier, and he never came out."

"Did *anybody* come out? Anyone moving furniture, laundry, carpets . . . ?"

"Nothing like that. Three people come out in the time you're talking about, well, six, to be precise. We had . . ." He reversed to the beginning of the footage. "Ten minutes after eleven. This guy who's come to collect a visitor of Mrs. Graham's, on the seventh."

There was a slightly distorted image of a man perhaps in his early thirties entering the elevator, pushing a wheelchair with an old woman in it. A moment later, they disembarked, and he wheeled her across the lobby and out into the street.

"Then half past eleven, Mr. Hofstadter and a friend of his got in. I thought at first his friend might be your partner. He's about the right size and build. But . . ."

He trailed off and shrugged. The porter said, "Mr. Hofstadter's been in the building twenty years . . ."

Dehan peered at the image and decided it was inconclusive, but unlikely. The guard went on. "Then we got eleven fifty-five. Mrs. Petersen from the fifth floor and her sister. We can keep looking . . ."

"I want copies of that footage . . . Go back. To eleven o'clock. Five past. This guy went to Mrs. Graham on the seventh?"

"Yeah, this is just the footage of people leaving, but . . ."

"Call her."

"What?"

"*Call her! Ask her if she had a disabled visitor, goddamn it!*"

The porter ran to reception. "I'll call!"

"Now, replay it . . . Freeze it. There. Look at the digital display. What's that number?"

"Holy shit . . ."

"It's a nine. That old woman in the wheelchair is my partner."

The porter poked his head in. "I am so sorry. She didn't have a visitor, and nobody came with a wheelchair . . ."

"Isolate that footage, send it to this email." She handed him a card and turned to the porter. "Tell me you saw a van. Tell me you saw a vehicle. Tell me you saw which way they went."

The man's face was a picture of distress. "I . . . He wheeled him out. I stayed in here. He might have turned right . . ."

She pulled her cell from her pocket and dialed the inspector.

"Carmen!"

"Sir, he was wheeled out of here at ten past eleven this morning, in a wheelchair. He was covered in a couple of blankets and a hat, to make him look like an old lady. I'm having the footage sent over, maybe the lab can do something with it, but the guy doing the wheeling is nondescript and hard to identify."

Though even as she was saying it, something was nagging at her memory. She went on.

"We need another team to canvass the area for anyone who saw a man pushing a wheelchair. They must have got into a vehicle. Someone might be able to identify the vehicle, or tell us which way it went."

"Dear God, Carmen. It is hard to believe. Who would do such a thing?"

She nodded. "Somebody crazy. I'm going out to talk to the neighbors."

She stepped out into the late-afternoon sunshine. The part of Riverside Drive where Penelope had her apartment was largely a residential area, and what few stores and businesses there were were mainly inside the buildings, and had no large plate glass storefronts that allowed a clear view of the street. So the first fifteen minutes of Dehan's hunt for witnesses was largely fruitless, until she came to the Upper West Side Cooperative School on West 96th, around the corner from Penelope's apartment block.

The school was closed, but, as she approached, beyond the iron railings she could see an elderly man in blue overalls with a wheelbarrow, tending to a small plot where a cherry tree was in blossom, surrounded by springtime flowerbeds. She took out her badge and held it through the rails, then stuck her fingers in her mouth and emitted a shrill whistle that might have shattered glass.

The guy straightened and turned. She waved her badge at him and called out, "Detective Dehan, NYPD!"

He ambled over to her and leaned on the green rails. He smiled without malice and said, "Dehan, huh? What's a nice girl like you doing in an outfit like that?"

"What can I tell you? My first choice was ballet, but my toes were too long. Were you here at eleven this morning?"

"Sure. I been here all day."

"I'm looking for witnesses who saw a man in his late twenties, early thirties, wheeling an old woman in a wheelchair. You see anything like that?"

"Yeah, sure. She was a weird-lookin' woman too. Big. That woman made some man's life a misery, I'm tellin' you. At the time she looked quiet, like maybe she was sleeping. He wheels her up the hill. You could tell she was heavy, 'cause this kid was struggling. Big hands, big feet. The woman, not the kid. Looked like a man, only she had this floppy hat with flowers on it. You wouldn't want to marry a woman like that."

"Where'd they go?"

"He had a van parked right there, across the road. Wheeled the chair into the van and secured it. Then drove away, like he was headed for the Hudson Parkway."

"You didn't get the plates . . . ?"

"Nah. They was odd, you know? An odd couple. But I didn't think it was nothin' criminal."

"You said the guy pushing was a kid?"

He made a rueful smile. "At my age, everyone's a kid. I guess he was what you said, late twenties, early thirties, medium height, medium build, kinda hard to describe. He was so normal."

"What kind of van was it?"

"White Savana, tinted windows. Had a side door with a ramp, to get the chair up." A cloud seemed to pass over the man's face. "He gonna hurt that woman?"

"That's what I'm trying to avoid. That woman is a six-foot-two mensch who also happens to be my partner and my husband."

"I'm sorry to hear that, Detective Dehan. I guess he'd make a better husband than a wife."

"Yeah, he makes a pretty good husband. Any distinguishing

features on the van? Anything to make it stand out from other white Savanas . . . ?"

He shrugged and looked momentarily helpless. "It was real clean. Actually, spotless. But there were no logos, no stickers, nothin'. All white with tinted windows. That's it."

"Tinted windows?"

"Yeah, along the back."

She nodded. "Okay, thanks."

"Hope you find him, Detective Dehan."

She turned and walked down the road, back toward Penelope's apartment block. On the way she put out a BOLO for the van. It was a forlorn hope, but it was something. Then she called Inspector Newman again.

"Carmen, what news?"

"He was loaded into a white Savana on West Ninety-Sixth by a man in his late twenties or early thirties. Medium height, medium build, nondescript. I put out a BOLO on the van. We'll need the CCTV footage from the Upper West Side Cooperative School on West Ninety-Sixth, also the neighboring streets. Maybe we can get a license plate and see where he was going. Seems he was headed for the Hudson Parkway."

"I'll take care of that, Carmen. What are you going to do?"

"I'm going to talk to Penelope again. Sir? Can you take Consuelo off the search for decapitated bodies and get her searching for vehicles registered to Penelope Peach, Grant Shaw, Alornerk Smith in Boston, and Helena Magnusson, also Shaw Line and Connors Communication. I want to see if that throws up any white Savanas."

"Of course, good thinking. Listen, Carmen, I really want you to consider taking a new partner for the remainder of this case."

"Sir, I'll take care of it myself if you are too busy . . ."

"Don't be impertinent, Carmen. That was not my point. You need support!"

"I need Stone, sir."

He sighed. "Very well. I'll see to this."

"Thank you, sir."

She made her way back to the unmarked Dodge, climbed behind the wheel, and, as the light started to fade in the city, drove back north along the banks of the Hudson. All the way she kept her mind focused and her emotions tightly battened down. Grief, despair, and fear cost lives. A clear, focused mind might be the only thing standing between Stone and death.

A white van.

Would a killer as methodical and systematic as this one have kept his van for five years? It was unlikely. What was not unlikely was that it was a taunt. A mockery. He, or she, had wanted the van to be seen. That was why he had parked it outside the school, where he could be certain it would be seen. He *wanted* it to be seen.

He or she.

Why? Why would he want the van to be seen? She stopped and corrected herself. "Stone would tell you that question is too open, Carmencita. Rephrase it. What would make him want the van to be seen?"

There was the taunt and the mockery, but this killer was smarter than that. This killer took out Jack Connors five years ago and had not been caught since. No, there was something more to it than taunting and mockery.

"Stone would say," she said aloud, "if he wanted the van to be seen, it was because he wanted to draw attention to it. What would make him want to draw attention to the van? Think, Carmen! *Think!*"

Her phone rang.

"Dehan."

"Detective Dehan, it's Consuelo. You wanted me to look into vehicles . . ."

"Yeah. What have you got?"

"Of the list of people and companies you gave me, Shaw Line Defense have a fleet of six white Savanas. They are of the passenger type. Do you want me to arrange to go and see them?"

"No, not yet. Good work. Anybody else?"

"Yes, it's a bit odd. I mean, I know it's a popular van, but Connors Communication own two and Alornerk Smith, in Boston, he also has one. Statistically, I think it's unlikely that so many of the people on your list would own the same vehicle."

"I agree. Get me the license plates on all of them. Then I want each one of those vans accounted for. Inform the inspector."

"I'm on it."

She hung up and pounded the wheel with her fist three times. Then she called ahead to have Penelope taken up to the interrogation room again.

Ten minutes later, she screeched to a halt outside the station, pushed through the door, and sprinted up the steps. She met Mo coming down, and for once in his life, he looked sincere.

"Carmen, I heard about Stone, I'm sorry . . ."

"Save it for the funeral, Mo."

She left him staring after her and ran the rest of the way to the top floor, where she burst into the interrogation room and bent over the table, staring down into Penelope's face.

"The van you saw, the one you thought was stalking you, was it a passenger vehicle?"

Penelope goggled. "What?"

"Did it have windows in the back? Yes or no?"

"No!"

"Are you sure?"

"Yes!"

"God*damn it!*" She turned and wrenched open the door again. Over her shoulder she snarled, "Get out of here! Go home!"

"What?"

"Get out! Go!"

From there she crossed to the inspector's office, hammered once, and went in.

"Carmen."

"Sir. I am letting Penelope go. Stone was right not to bring her in. She was stalked by a white van just before Jack was killed. The white van that stalked her had no windows in the back. This van has windows. It was parked outside just about the only place in that neighborhood where it was sure to be seen by witnesses. That means Stone's abductor *wanted* the van to be seen. He wanted the van to be seen because he wanted us to connect it with Grant Shaw and the original white van Penelope saw five years ago. Shaw uses a fleet of white Savanas. So it could not have been Shaw or Penelope. This guy—this person—is very, very clever at deflecting suspicion and staying *out* of the picture."

"Consuelo told me about the vans. I've sent a car to check on the vehicles and establish their whereabouts this morning. What about the other two?"

"Alornerk and Jack's own company, Connors Communication. They own three vans between them, all fitting the description by the witness. Alornerk certainly had motive to kill Jack. I don't see him abducting Stone and setting up this elaborate show, but he's a mathematician, right? And an academic. They're all crazy. I need to find out where he was today. Maybe we can call Boston PD and have them send somebody over to ask him. Come to think of it, he should have come in today to make a statement."

"Interesting."

"Yeah. Meantime, that leaves two vans belonging to Jack's own company, and I have to tell you, sir, that, to me, stinks like shit soup. Excuse me."

"You'd better explain."

She shook her head. "Right back to first principles, Chief: who benefited from his death? Helena. And not only did she benefit, he was screwing another chick who was younger and better looking. Okay, so Helena was also screwing another guy. But she wasn't in love with him. All along, the man she loved was Jack. And Jack barely knew she existed and treated her like shit."

He frowned. "The person in the CCTV footage is a man."

"And the one in the wheelchair is an old woman. And yet." She shook her head again. "That is not hard to arrange, sir, and besides, she may have an accomplice, a younger man to do the heavy lifting. She is an attractive, very rich woman with a lot of admirers and followers. It would not be hard for her . . ."

She frowned and became momentarily distracted. The inspector was nodding. "Indeed—Alornerk himself! Well, we should know shortly if Connors Communications' vans were used today, and if so, by whom. What is it, Carmen? Something wrong?"

"I just remembered . . ."

There was a tap at the door and the inspector snapped, "Come!"

A uniform poked his head in and said, "Detective Dehan, you have a UPS delivery. Maria signed for it and it's on your desk."

"Yeah, thanks . . ."

She stared at the inspector. He stared back.

In a strange trance, she moved out of the office, hearing only the blood in her ears. She moved down the stairs and pushed into the detectives' room. Everybody was staring at her, though she was not aware of them. She was aware only of the carton standing on her desk, eighteen inches cubed, and Stone's empty chair beyond it.

SIXTEEN

THE INSPECTOR PUSHED PAST HER IN A RUSH.

"Carmen, let me open it. Somebody take Carmen away from here! For God's sake, get her out of here!"

Mo stepped toward her; Consuelo, who had been working at Dehan's desk, rose and moved toward her, arms stretched out.

Dehan snarled, "Stay away from me! Don't touch that box!"

She reached in her jeans and pulled out a blade. She advanced on the box and, with her hands shaking badly, she cut the tape and gripped the cardboard flaps. The detectives had gathered around her. The inspector stepped forward, reaching for her. "Carmen, no . . ."

"*Stay away!*"

Her face was pale and drawn, and with sudden vicious violence she ripped open the box, stared inside, and screamed. She staggered back a step, covering her face, and fell into her chair, still screaming. Then she was on her feet, pounding the desk with her fist. She kicked her chair and sent it crashing against the wall. "*Motherfucker!*"

She turned and stared at the rows of astonished faces watching her. "*What are you all staring at? He's not in there! He hasn't had his fucking head cut off!*"

Mo was the first to move, then the small crowd began to disperse. The deputy inspector stepped toward her and held her shoulders. She stared into his face, her own a sickly gray color, biting back the sobs, blinking away the tears, her hands trembling.

"Carmen, put the knife away."

She folded it and put it in her pocket.

"Sit down. Somebody, Consuelo, get her a coffee. Now just take a moment to breathe and get a grip. It was not him, and that is a good thing, right?"

"Don't even dream about taking me off this case, sir."

"It's okay, just take it easy. Nobody's taking you off anything. But we need to get this stuff to the lab."

"Not yet." She stood, took some latex gloves from her jacket pocket, and pulled them on. "There's a note, and I saw a photograph."

She reached in the box, which was almost empty, and extracted an envelope and a photograph of a dense woodland. She examined the photograph a moment and handed it to the inspector. Then she opened the envelope and read aloud in a steady voice.

"'No head for you today, Detective Dehan. Your husband is intact, but buried in a shallow grave. I guess I could have googled it, but I just didn't have the interest: How long can a person survive buried alive?'" She paused, hesitated, then continued. "'Do I seem cruel? Yet I am trying to redeem myself. At least I spared him the cheese cutter and gave him a chance. Hurry now! You might just find him in time.'"

The room seemed to rock under her feet. She reached out to the deputy inspector with fumbling fingers and took back the photograph. It was a glade in a forest. It meant nothing to her. She forced herself to focus. The ground was dark and mulchy: last fall's leaves rotted into the soil. A large tree stood in the center of the picture, perhaps an oak, maybe fifteen or twenty feet from the camera, with large ferns on the right and more trees she could not identify. To the left, her left, a space between trees showed a patch of water. And in the foreground, near the foot of the oak, a mound where the earth had been disturbed.

She handed it back to the inspector. "We need to have this copied to all the sheriff's departments, Jersey to Maine, parks authorities, every cop in every PD on the East Coast. Somebody knows where this is."

He took the picture. "Consuelo, see to it. Copy it to every cell phone in the Forty-Third, then get it out to every precinct in New York State, copy it to the sheriff's departments, park authorities—everyone and anyone you can think of. There is an NYPD detective buried alive at this spot, we need to know where it is *now*!"

He turned back to Dehan. She was already talking over him. "He's had him maybe six hours. Allow for the time to dig the ground, put him in the hole, drive back, prepare the package, and have it delivered. That limits him to an area of less than three hours from the Upper West Side."

"Much less, Carmen, two to two and a half maximum."

"Okay, now, much of that is through the city, where his speed is going to be limited to twenty or thirty miles per hour . . ."

"Until he hits the freeway, when his speed will increase to double that, assuming he sticks to the speed limit."

"So we are looking in a circumference of about a hundred miles."

"That is millions of acres of woodland . . ."

"Madison is a hundred miles away. The other bodies were found on the route to Madison . . ."

"Penelope again? Carmen . . ."

She shook her head. "No. It's a red herring. Why didn't he decapitate Stone? That box was intended for his head, but it wasn't in it."

He shook his head, frowning. "I don't know . . ."

"What *stopped* him from cutting off his head? He told us what. He told us he was seeking redemption. It's a long shot, sir, but if he abducted Stone intending to cut off his head, but then refrained from decapitating him, that has to mean that something during that brief period of five or six hours made him change his mind, right? What happened during that time? We don't know; perhaps they talked, perhaps Stone got inside his head."

"Perhaps . . ."

"Whatever it was, it means that the decision to bury him in a shallow grave instead of decapitating him came later. Which means he had less time to drive out and back, which places the woodland closer to home."

"All right, that's good."

"Now, dense woodland within New York is mainly in the Bronx . . ."

Mo had got up from his desk and approached, listening to her. A couple of other detectives had stopped what they were doing to listen. She went on. "What have we got? We've got Pugsley Creek Park, Soundview Park . . ."

Mo snapped his fingers and pointed at her. "The Botanical Gardens! The Thain Family Forest. You got a river in that picture, the Bronx River flows right through it."

"Yes!"

The inspector turned to the room and started hollering, "All right! I want every available officer in the briefing room in two minutes! Drop whatever you are doing! Go! We are organizing search parties! In the briefing room *now*!"

There was a flurry of activity as uniforms and plain clothes alike converged on the briefing room. Dehan did not join them. Her mind was racing, and she was staring at her laptop, scouring a map of the Botanical Gardens, trying to put herself in the killer's mind, asking herself not where *she* would bury a body, but where she would bury a body if she was this particular killer.

She found there were not that many places you could enter the park in seclusion. Logic dictated Stone was either conscious or unconscious, dead or alive. If he was unconscious or dead, he would have to be transported in some way. If he was conscious, he would probably be made to walk, with a gun in his back. Either way, most entrances to the park were on main roads with lots of public access, and the risk of discovery was high. The only access point she could find that was more or less remote was southbound on the Bronx River Parkway, just after the Williams Bridge, where a short road led down from the bridge to feed into the highway. There, there was a small patch of wasteland by the railway, at the very tip of the Botanical Gardens. There you could take in your van, park it in the cover of the trees, and either walk your victim or push them in a wheelchair down the secluded path where few visitors to the park would go, then veer off the track and in among the trees. And there, right there, was the river.

She grabbed her jacket and ran. She paused just a moment at the front desk.

"Maria, tell the chief I went to the north end of the Botanical Gardens."

"Find him."

"You bet your sweet ass I will!"

It was a short drive. She picked up the Bronx River Parkway on Story Avenue, set the siren howling, and hit a hundred going north. In less than five minutes, she was slowing to come off onto the Williams Bridge. There she did a U and came down off the bridge onto the slip road, where she found the patch of wasteland and pulled off.

Late afternoon was shifting to evening. The shadows of the trees were long and dense in the copper light. She grabbed the flashlight from the trunk and set off at a steady jog along the path, keeping the river on her right and scanning the clearings for anything that was reminiscent of the photograph.

Soon the river began to recede, and she was forced to slow to a walk and move in among the woodland, into the shadows and the dark, trying to keep the river in view. Darkness closed in. The hum and hiss of the traffic faded until the only sound was the croak of the frogs and the lap of the water, and her own feet treading on the dead leaves and the dry twigs underfoot. The failing light and the heavy shadows made it increasingly hard to identify the clearing, but in her mind, the large oak tree was vivid, and she knew that when she saw it, she would know it.

But she didn't see it. She pressed on, going ever deeper into the forest, following the course of the river, keeping the water at roughly the distance it had been in the picture. But as she moved on, the ferns grew more dense, the trees more massive and more thickly grouped, the terrain ever harder to negotiate, until eventually she was trudging ankle-deep through mud and sludge, clambering over giant roots, unable to see more than a few yards ahead of herself. Finally she stopped and realized that she was completely lost, and it was totally dark.

She played the flashlight around the trees. Even if she had seen the tree, now she doubted she would recognize it. A twist of despair and panic gripped her gut and a wave of nausea washed over her. She should have brought a team with her. She should have waited for the inspector to finish his briefing. But the panic, the urgency to find him had blinded her.

She reached for her phone, intending to call for backup, but a noise made her stop. An animal perhaps, a small, feral predator seeking food. She stood motionless, listening, trying to rein in her imagination. Had she been led here? Had she been drawn here so the killer could get her too? It was irrational. How could the killer have known she would come without backup? How could he have known she would come at all? How could he, or she, know that Dehan would be there alone?

The noise came again: a large body pushing through undergrowth. A crack of a dry branch under a heavy foot. Then silence.

Dehan killed the flashlight, pulled her piece, and backed away from the noise into the cover of a large tree. Behind her, to her right, she could hear the lap and splash of the river. On her left were tall, thick ferns. Ahead, just beyond the clearing, there was a gap in the trees and what looked like a narrow footpath. She crouched down and leveled her gun at the gap, and waited.

A shadow, darker than the shadows around it, shifted near the footpath. She narrowed her eyes, unsure if it had been a moving branch or a body. Another shift and then a pale reflection, like skin, a face half-seen among the shadows of the leaves.

She took aim and shouted, "NYPD! Identify yourself! Step into the clearing!"

Nothing happened for a moment. Then there was another rustle, as of a body moving among branches and foliage. The pallid face became clearer, dancing disembodied among the shadows.

She shouted again, "This is the New York Police Department! Identify yourself!" Another step forward.

The face drew closer, staring blindly ahead, as though suspended from the branches above. It stopped. Sick panic gripped her. It was impossible in the darkness of the forest to make out any body beneath the head. It seemed to hang, gaping in the air. A voice, a hoarse whisper, filtered through the undergrowth above the ripple of the stream and the croak of the frogs. "*Dehan? Is that you? Did you come . . . ?*"

She switched on the flashlight and stood, shouting, "*Identify yourself!*"

The funnel of light picked out a tall man. His clothes were dark gray or black. He held up his right arm to shield his eyes and took a step forward. Again he said, "Dehan? What the hell are you doing here?"

She stepped toward him, seeing now that his clothes were covered in slime and mud, recognizing his face in the light, smeared also with sludge and mire.

"Stone? Oh God, Stone!" She ran and hurled herself at him, taking him in her arms and crushing him to her. "*You're alive! Thank God you're alive!*"

He held on to her, leaned against her, and then fell to the ground. She knelt by his side, feeling for a pulse. It was faint, but there. She felt his hands and face. They were cold. She rubbed them hard, then grabbed her phone and called the inspector.

"Dehan! Where the hell are you? Why were you not at the briefing?"

"I have him, sir. I think he's going into hypothermia. He needs a doctor right now, and probably hospital. I am sending you my location. You need to come in off the Williams Bridge. Please hurry!"

"You *have* him? What in the name of . . . ? Is he okay? Where *are* you?"

"Sir? Can we talk later? Just get here, please!"

"All right! All right! We're on our way."

He hung up, and she sent him her location. Then she wrapped Stone in her jacket and began to slap and pat his face until he slowly came around again.

"Stone? Stone! I know you're tired. I know you want to sleep. But you have to do this for me, okay? You need to stand up. I'll support you. I'll hold you, but you need to stand up and you need to walk. We need to walk to the car, okay? I'm going to take you home and get you warm. Come on, big fella, get *up*!"

He struggled, and she heaved him to his feet, hooking his arm over her shoulder. He swayed and groaned but stayed upright. Then they staggered, one step at a time, toward the footpath, where they turned left and headed slowly through the dense shadows and the looming trees back toward the Charger, and home.

"I knew you'd come," he said.

"You bet your ass you knew. You owe me six kids and a retirement home in Madison, remember."

They staggered on. "I remember," he said.

SEVENTEEN

WHEN I WOKE UP, I WASN'T SURE WHO I WAS, AND I HAD no idea where I was. I knew I wasn't where I had been. I had been in a cellar, and there had been a wire across my throat. My hands and feet had been tied so hard I couldn't move them. I couldn't remember how I had got there. But I knew that was where I had been.

Before.

Then it had been dark and wet, and I couldn't move and I couldn't breathe. I felt the thrash of panic inside me and took deep breaths, long, slow, deep breaths. That was before. Now I was okay.

I was in a room in a hospital. The walls were white. There was a TV up on the wall that was switched off. On my right there was a white door with a clipboard hanging on a hook. On my left there was a window with panoramic views of New York. As I looked, I realized that I knew the area. It was Morris Park. I lived in Morris Park.

Right beside my bed, beneath the window, was a large armchair, and in the chair was Dehan. Dehan was asleep and looked extremely beautiful. She was my wife; my wife and my partner.

I was a cop.

A detective. I was Detective John Stone, NYPD. And my partner in the chair was Carmen Dehan. I smiled and sat like that for maybe twenty minutes, looking out at the spring sunshine while she slept. Slowly things came back to me, piecemeal, but not a whole picture, and the thing that filled my mind the most was the cold, wet mud clinging to my face and my body, clogging my mouth and my nose.

After a while, I realized that Dehan had her eyes open and was watching me. She smiled at me.

"Hey, big guy."

"Hi."

"How are you feeling?"

"Pretty confused. How long have I been here?"

She looked at her watch. "About fifteen hours. How much do you remember?"

I shook my head. "Bits, pieces. It's like it's downloading but I have a modem from the nineties."

She frowned. "Really? What do you mean?"

I pointed at my head. "There are big, empty spaces, mainly about . . ." I paused. "Last night? The last couple of days."

She stood and came to sit on my bed. She took my hand. It felt good. "What's the last thing you remember, Stone?"

"I was in a cellar. I was tied to a table, on my back. There was somebody there, but I couldn't see them. They put . . ." I hesitated, an enormous sleepiness overwhelming me. I fought it, looked into Dehan's eyes, and drew strength. "They put a cheese wire across my throat that was attached to a pulley."

She closed her eyes for a moment and gripped my hand. When she'd opened them again she asked, "They? There was more than one of them?"

I shook my head. "There was only one. It's hard to remember. Most of the time it was dark. I remember a black dress, black stockings, blond hair pulled back . . . It was . . ."

"A woman?"

"I remember a woman." I sighed and shook my head. "I'm sorry, Dehan. That's all I remember."

"It wasn't Penelope."

"Penelope . . ."

"You remember Penelope?" She said it like there was a "surely" tacked on the front. I stared out the window.

After a while, I said, "Madison. But she had an apartment in the city. Upper West Side, Riverside Drive."

"Jesus, Stone! You remember the case?"

I stared at her for a long time. "Jack Connors? He was beheaded. Somebody cut off his head . . ."

"You have amnesia. Holy sh . . ."

"I'm sorry, Dehan."

"Don't be stupid. It's not your fault. I can't even imagine what you've been through. I'll call the doctor."

She left the room, and I lay staring out the window, seeing not the trees or the fresh blue sky but the darkness of my memories, and the impenetrable black spaces between them.

Jack Connors. He was in advertising. He'd gone out to lunch . . . No, not to lunch, to meet Penelope. He was going to her apartment. Like me. I went to her apartment. I was in her apartment, talking to her. She had lied, and cried. She was skilled at manipulating people's emotions—men's emotions. Had Jack gone there and spoken to her, like me?

I had left. Had he left too? I had left to go back to Dehan. Why had he left?

The door opened, and Dehan came in with a young, balding man in jeans and a white coat. He looked like a butcher, only he had a stethoscope around his neck that proclaimed him a doctor.

"Good morning, Detective Stone, how are we feeling this morning?"

"Great. Can you answer a question for me?"

"Ask me the question and I'll tell you if I can answer it." He smiled like he'd said something funny and also wise.

I returned the smile and asked, "Why do doctors always talk in the first-person plural?"

He laughed like I was a loveable old rogue. "I guess it's a misguided attempt to create rapport. How are *you* feeling, Detective?"

Rapport.

"I feel fine, tired but good. I have big holes in my memory, though." He frowned, and I ignored him. "Rapport, is that an NLP thing?"

Now he looked surprised. "NLP?"

"Yeah, I read somewhere if you mirror a person, make them identify with you by the things you say and do, you will create rapport, and they will be easier to persuade."

He shook his head. "No, it's just one of those old bedside manner things. I am more interested in the holes in your memory. It's not unusual after a traumatic experience to have a certain amount of amnesia. I don't want you forcing your memory, Detective. The most likely thing is that it will come back in dribs and drabs all on its own, but if you force it, it will have the contrary effect. In any case, I am going to arrange for you to see a psychologist who specializes in trauma-induced amnesia."

He made a note on a clipboard he was holding, and while he was writing, he asked me, "What is the last thing you remember?"

"I was in a cellar. I felt a bit high, like I'd been given something. The walls were bare brick. There was a lot of junk in boxes, there were steps leading up to a door, a bulb hanging from the ceiling. I was tied to a table with nylon rope, and there was a wire, like a piano wire, or a cheese cutter, across my throat, attached to a pulley on my right."

Dehan went to the window, and the doctor sat on a chair beside the bed. "Don't strain yourself. If you feel at all distressed . . ."

"I'm okay. I want to remember. There was somebody there. The light was poor, and my sight was kind of foggy, but I could make out a black dress, black stockings, blond hair pulled back in a kind of loose knot."

Dehan turned to look down at me. "A woman."

I nodded. "I remember recognizing her. I knew who she was."

"But you don't now?"

"I'm trying, but it's like a wall, like my mind doesn't want to go there."

"Then don't." It was the doctor. "Just rest and take it easy. Our resident psychiatrist will be around to see you later on. For now, I want you to *rest*." He glanced at Dehan. "Understood?"

She nodded, but her face was expressionless. I said, "Understood."

He gave me a quick physical, made a note on my chart, and left. Dehan sat on the bed and took hold of my hand. I studied her face for a while, marveling, not for the first time, at how lucky I was. After a bit, I asked her, "Where did you find me?"

"The Botanical Gardens. Do you have any recollection of how you got there?"

I shook my head. "I remember feeling panic. I remember a heavy weight on my body and my limbs, mud on my face. Then I remember the darkness of the woods, trying to walk. It was like a dream: a nightmare. If somebody told me I had dreamed it, I'd believe them. Then you."

She squeezed my hand. "She, this woman, sent a note. There was a photograph of where you were buried, and a note saying she hadn't killed you because she was looking for redemption."

I frowned and closed my eyes. The word seemed to echo inside my head. It had meaning. I had spoken to her.

"I spoke to her. I told her to release me, to cut the bonds and take the wire from my throat. I told her it wasn't too late to make it right."

Do it now and I promise you, I will help you find redemption.

"I told her, I said, 'Do it now and I will help you find redemption.'"

"Son of a gun."

"I told her I knew there were others. Did they find any others?"

"Yeah, two, both on the road to Madison."

"Madison?" I frowned. "That doesn't make sense. Torso or head?"

"Torso. Why doesn't it make sense?"

"I'm not sure. But it wasn't Penelope, Dehan, or Shaw."

"You're remembering."

"Shaw was her lover, but she was in love with Jack." I closed my eyes again and spoke like I was in a trance. "Jack was in love with her too. They were in love with each other, they were going to get married. She promised him she would break up with Shaw, and she did, that night." I opened my eyes. "She didn't have sex with Shaw that night. They broke up on good terms, as friends. She called Jack the next day to tell him she'd broken up with him and he went to her apartment, only . . ." I sat up, memories begin-ning to flood back. "Only it *wasn't* like me! He never arrived. He never arrived, so he never left. He must have been picked up before he got there." My mind was racing. I began snapping my fingers, like the clicking would make the memories come faster. "I was coming back to you, but he wasn't going back to anybody. It was Penelope he wanted to be with. He wasn't going back to . . ." I stared into Dehan's face. "Helena . . ."

"Jesus Christ . . ."

"The black dress and the stockings of a wife in mourning, the blond hair pulled back in a knot, that was who I remembered. It was Helena."

Dehan pulled her phone from her pocket and dialed. After a moment she said, "Consuelo, Dehan here . . . You called last night? I was pretty tied up. Did you chase up the vans at Connors Communication? Oh, that was what you were calling about? Good, okay, shoot . . . That's great. Good work. Later." She hung up and sighed. "Connors Communication own two white Savanas."

"That's significant?"

"You were seen being wheeled out of Penelope's block in a wheelchair yesterday at eleven a.m. You had been roughly disguised as an old woman."

"Great."

"You were taken around to 96th Street, where there was a white Savana waiting. You were loaded in and driven away. Connors Communication own two such vans. One of them was taken out yesterday by Penelope."

I scratched my head. I was beginning to get a headache. "Surely there is CCTV footage . . ."

"There is."

"So who was wheeling me?"

"It *looks* like a young man, but you know what CCTV is like. The quality is not great, and hell, *you* look like an old woman. Only, you know, you don't, big guy." She grinned and winked, which kind of helped, but not a lot.

"You think it could be Helena?"

She shrugged. "I don't know. Honestly, I don't. The techs are on it as we speak. Either way." She shrugged and walked to the window. "Thinking about it, she is a woman who has a way of fascinating men. She had enough fans and disciples, it's not impossible she could have roped one of them in. Hell, Stone!" She turned to face me again. "She's a crime writer. This is literally her daily bread."

"Disciples."

"What?"

"One of her disciples."

"One of her students, a fan, Jesus, even Alornerk. Men seemed to fall for her. What's wrong?"

I had swung my legs out of bed. "We need to go and take her in."

"You're not going anywhere, Stone."

"I am going to Helena Magnusson's house to take her into custody, and you are coming with me."

"No way! You are staying in bed, and I will go and take her in. Don't be an ass, Stone!"

"Don't upset me. I have had a rough couple of days. Get me my pants."

"I said, no way!"

"Fine." I stood and made my way across the room to the wardrobe.

"Goddamn it, Stone!"

"This is simple, Dehan. You help me or I do it alone. But unless you plan to physically assault me and tie me to the bed, a thing I have frankly had just about enough of over the last couple of days, I am going to Helena Magnusson's house and I am going to take her into custody. So get with the program, kid!"

"I swear! One of these days!"

"Shut up, Dehan, and help me get dressed."

She glared at me, wrenched my clothes from the wardrobe, and snapped, "Sit down!"

Ten minutes later, she was climbing behind the wheel of the Jag, and I was getting in the passenger seat beside her. As we pulled out of the lot, I called Dispatch and asked for backup. When we had turned onto the Hutchinson River Parkway headed south, she said, "Okay, talk me through this."

I knew what was going to happen next, so I smiled at her and waited. She sniffed, gave her head a small twitch, and went on.

"Helena Magnusson and Jack Connors kept up the public image of being very much in love and happily married. It was good for each of their public images. But in fact they had been growing apart for some time. He had been seeing Penelope for a while, and they had been gradually falling in love. Helena had been seeing Alornerk, but for her it was more an act of revenge against a man who—or as you would say, whom—she still loved and was not ready to let go of, but who had betrayed her."

"Sounds about right."

"Shut up."

I smiled. "You asked me to talk you through it."

"Shut up. So, bit by bit, Jack's relationship with Penelope turns from an affair, to infatuation, to being actually pretty serious, to the point where he is prepared to leave his wife and she is ready to dump the guys who have been keeping her. Somehow Helena finds out. Maybe she finds some texts, gets into his email, hears them on the phone, all of the above, or maybe it's just good old female intuition. Whatever the case, she finds out, and she decides to kill him. One thing is having an affair, quite another is getting serious and planning to dump her and marry another, younger woman.

"So, when he calls to say he is going out to lunch, she knows that this is code for, 'I am going to see Penny,' and she goes to wait for him. When he comes out of his office onto the street, she intercepts him. Maybe she tells him she knows where he is going, maybe she uses some other excuse; either way, neither of them wants a public scene, so he gets in the car. Once in the car, either alone or with the help of an accomplice, she knocks him out and drives him to their house. From there she takes him to their basement, where we are going to find the setup you described. She straps him down and cuts off his head." She glanced at me. "Sorry if this is a bit close to home."

"It's fine. Go right ahead."

"She then packages up the head and sends it to herself at the college, by UPS, where she will receive it in a very public fashion and thus become the victim and so the least likely suspect. Meanwhile, Alornerk, her accomplice, provides her with her alibi. The really brilliant part of the plan is that her alibi works on two levels. If the first alibi is busted, she has the perfect excuse, which also provides her with a second alibi. A plan worthy of a novelist of her caliber."

"Question."

"Shoot."

"What about the other bodies? What made her kill them?

Also, why did we find the bodies and not the heads? Why were the heads not mailed to anybody?"

She stared at me for a moment, then shrugged. "I guess we're about to find out."

"I guess we are."

EIGHTEEN

WE TURNED INTO WEST 122ND OFF MORNINGSIDE Avenue with two patrol cars hot on our tails and pulled up outside Helena's front door. I climbed out with care while Dehan bounded up the steps, leaned on the bell, and hammered on the wood. The patrolmen stood on the sidewalk and watched us. I climbed the steps. Dehan looked at me.

"We need to get a warrant."

I shook my head and pulled my Swiss Army knife from my pocket. I hammered it into the lock with the heel of my hand and opened the door. "I think Alornerk is in here murdering her. And I thought I heard a scream."

She looked down at the patrolmen. "You guys heard that?"

They shrugged. One of them said, "The traffic . . ."

I stepped into the hall with my badge in my hand and shouted, "Detectives John Stone and Carmen Dehan, NYPD! Helena Magnusson! Are you here? Ebba?"

There was utter stillness and silence in the house. Dehan had her weapon in her hand. I turned to the uniforms. "Hart, I want you on the door. Nobody comes in, nobody goes out. The other three, upstairs. Don't touch anything. If you find a person, detain them and call me."

"You got it, Detective."

The other three climbed the stairs, weapons drawn. We moved into a formal drawing room. It was empty, tidy, and clean. The cushions on the chairs and the sofa were all fluffed; the glasses and decanters were unused. There was no indication that anybody had been there in the last twenty-four hours.

From there we moved into the dining room. It was the same. The table was clean and polished. It looked like a room in a museum. We moved through it to the kitchen. It was modern, with a black-and-white tiled floor, a gigantic silver fridge, an island with a huge iron range built into it, and a sofa and two armchairs up against the far wall set around a coffee table. On the coffee table there was a coffeepot and a single cup. There was also an open magazine.

On the sofa, Ebba was sitting staring at us. She looked astonished, and strangely immobile. There was a neat, black hole in the middle of her forehead, and the wall behind her head was a mess of gore and blood that had begun to dry.

I pulled my cell from my pocket. I said to Dehan, "Tell the guys this is now a crime scene. Have Hart seal the place off and see what they've got upstairs. I'll call this in."

She left the kitchen; I made the call and had a look around. There was nothing. Nothing I could latch on to and work from. She had been sitting having coffee and reading a magazine. Somebody had come into the kitchen and shot her. Somebody who was already in the house, otherwise she would have had to get up to answer the door.

I pulled latex gloves from my pocket and put them on, then made my way back through the drawing room, past the front door where Hart was putting up the yellow tape, and up the stairs to the bedrooms and the morning room where she had received us on the first day. Dehan was there looking around. As I came in, she said, "The ashes in the fire are still warm, but not hot. The cushions on one of the chairs have been disturbed, and also on the sofa. There is a glass of sherry on the occasional table beside the chair, but no other glasses anywhere else in the room. It looks like she was alone in here."

"Doesn't make much sense. She's sitting having a glass of sherry in front of the fire on her own. Suddenly she gets up, goes down to the kitchen, and shoots Ebba in the head with a nine-millimeter pistol. Then leaves."

"I've had a look for her purse or any form of ID. I can't find any. I told Hart and his partner to stay on the door. I told the other guys they could go."

"Okay." I nodded. "Ebba is downstairs in the kitchen. She's sitting drinking coffee and reading her magazine. So her killer is already in the house. There is no sign of struggle up here or in the drawing room downstairs, in the dining room . . ."

"Or in the bedrooms."

"There is no blood immediately apparent. What would make Helena . . ."

Hart stepped into the room. "Detectives, there is a neighbor downstairs who wants to talk to you. She says she saw Mrs. Magnusson leave with a man."

Dehan skipped down the stairs, and I followed more carefully, trying to ignore the blunt axe wedged in my skull and the waves of nausea that occasionally washed over me.

The woman at the door was tall, dressed in jeans and a Columbia sweatshirt. She was in her early thirties and had wide hips and narrow ankles, and her hair was piled up on her head like she thought she wasn't tall enough. Dehan approached her.

"Hi, I'm Detective Dehan; this is my partner, Detective Stone. You have some information for us about Helena Magnusson?"

She had the trick of talking as though she was asking questions. "Well, I'm guessing you're looking for her? She went out this morning? I was putting the kids in the car to take them to school? So that would be, like, seven thirty? She was with a man, and they were getting into her car, and I waved over to her. 'Cause you know? I don't often see her early like that? So I said, like, 'Hey, you're up early!' and she says, like, 'Yeah, I'm going away for a bit.' Like, you know, she was going away for a long time? Which I thought was strange 'cause she had no luggage, you know? So, you know, I don't know, like, when she's coming back."

I said, "Can you describe the man?"

She cocked a hip and sighed, staring up at the sky. "That's kinda hard because he was like one of those like nondescript guys? Kind of average height, average build, and he, like, got straight in the car? So I didn't really get a chance to look at him?"

Dehan asked, "Did she say where she was going?"

In the distance, we heard the wail of police sirens approaching. The woman glanced away up the street, then looked back at Dehan. "She said she was going back home. She said, one of those kinda Scandinavian countries: Switzerland? That's Scandinavia, right? Or Norway?"

I said, "Denmark?"

She nodded. "Yeah, Denmark. It was Denmark. That's right. She was going back home to Denmark."

I pulled my cell from my pocket. "Okay, Sergeant Hart here will take your statement. Thanks, you've been very helpful." I stepped out onto the stoop as two patrol cars, the crime scene van, and the ME's car came into the street and crowded around my Jag outside the door with their lights flashing.

Dehan was just behind me on her phone. She said, "I'm looking at morning departures, New York to Denmark. We have JFK Copenhagen, Norwegian Air, departed at eleven twenty this morning. Call, I'm still looking."

"That's the one." I called. It rang a couple of times. Frank climbed the steps, and Dehan took him inside. On the sidewalk, the CS team were climbing into their suits.

Then a man's voice said, "Norwegian, how can I help you?"

"This is Detective John Stone of the NYPD. I need your manifest for flight 7014 out of JFK for Copenhagen at eleven twenty this morning."

"Sure, of course I can do that. I will need your police email." I gave it to him and heard the rattle of keys. "Is there any particular passenger you are looking for?"

"Yeah. Helena Magnusson."

He rattled a little longer. "I have sent you the manifest, Detective Stone, and I can confirm that Helena Magnusson was booked on that flight, first class."

"Thanks."

I hung up. Dehan was on the doorstep looking at me. "What?"

"She was on the eleven twenty." My phone pinged. "That will be the flight manifest."

"Mother . . . ! What a stupid, pointless . . ."

"Yeah . . ."

"We'll have to start extradition proceedings. Who was the guy? Alornerk? I guess he'll be on the manifest too."

I shook my head. "He's not exactly nondescript or average height."

"She must be crazy. She let you go because she wanted redemption. Then she just goes right ahead, kills Ebba and flees the country? What's the sense in that?"

I stared at her for a long moment, nodded, and looked down the street to see the inspector's car turning in from Morningside Avenue. He pulled up behind my Jag, climbed out, and stood staring up at me for a moment. Then he sighed and climbed the stoop to stand in front of me.

"I am not a man inclined to swearing, John, but what the *hell* are you doing here?"

"Helena Magnusson has gone AWOL, sir. It looks as though she killed her maidservant before she left with a man. She was booked on the eleven twenty Norwegian Air flight to Copenhagen."

"Good Lord! What are you telling me?"

Dehan answered for me. "We were in the hospital, sir."

"Where you belong," he said to me, with some severity.

"Stone was, probably still is, suffering from partial amnesia.

But he began to remember bits, and it came to him that the person who abducted him was Helena Magnusson . . ."

"Are you *sure,* John?"

"He was drugged, sir, and his vision was blurry, but it looked like her, and . . ." She gestured at the house. "It is looking very much like she has murdered her maid and fled the country."

"But . . . *why?*"

I got in before Dehan. "Presumably because she feared that with this second investigation it would be discovered that she murdered her husband. It is the behavior of a very emotionally unstable person."

"So, she murdered her own husband, decapitated him, and mailed herself his head? Is that what you are telling me?"

Dehan shrugged. "It sounds crazy, sir, but then I guess decapitating people is pretty crazy in itself, right? She discovered that not only was he having an affair, but he was planning to leave her for Penelope Peach. Penelope had broken up with the man who was keeping her, and they had arranged to meet at Penelope's apartment. Only he never showed up, because Helena intercepted him, brought him here, and killed him. Mailing herself the head was the perfect way to deflect suspicion. Plus she had her lover provide her with an alibi."

She looked at me. "We'll have to pull him in, see to what extent he was involved. We should also go down to the basement and see if you recognize it."

The inspector frowned at Dehan, then at me. "You sure you feel up to that?"

I nodded. "Sure. I have a feeling it wasn't here anyway."

We followed the crime scene team into the kitchen. The door was beside the fridge. I opened it and flipped on the light. There was a long, narrow wooden staircase that descended eight or ten steps, then made a right angle down into an ample cellar with a concrete floor. There was a boiler, a washing machine and a dryer, the usual junk stashed up against one wall. The walls were bare brick, but there was no table, and there was no cheese cutter. I stood in the middle of the floor and shook my head.

"No. This is not the place."

The inspector frowned at me again. "Are you sure? You said you were drugged and your vision was blurry."

I shrugged. "I'm pretty sure this is not the place. We'll get the CS guys in to have a look, but the stairs are all wrong, there is no door. This isn't the place."

He sighed heavily. "Well, in any case, I guess we can start wrapping up the investigation and tying up the loose ends. It was a challenging case, and all credit to you for closing it. We'll request extradition from Denmark, but I don't hold out much hope. She'll disappear within the European Union and probably fly out east or to South America before we can get the bureaucratic machinery up and running." He patted my shoulder. "I'm sorry, John. It was a great job and you deserved to get your man. But I guess you can't win them all. There is always one that gets away."

"I guess so, sir."

Dehan made a face of ruefulness and smiled through it at me. "Funny how she warned us right from the start that it might be a woman . . ."

I grunted. "I thought she was hinting at Penelope."

The inspector adopted a paternal air. "Well, look, you two. I think you have done quite enough and you must be exhausted, especially you, John. There is nothing more for you to do here. I insist you go home and take a few days off. The crime scene team can take it from here. I'll ask Alor . . ."

"Alornerk."

"Thank you. I'll ask him to come in, and we'll question him in light of these new events. You can deal with that, Carmen, can't you, tomorrow or the day after? We can consider the case solved, if not yet fully closed. The rest is up to the lawyers. Now, off you go, home and rest."

We thanked him and made our way up the steps and through the kitchen, where Frank's boys were lifting poor Ebba onto a gurney and out onto the stoop. As we went carefully down the steps, I held out my hand. "Keys, please. I feel the need to drive the old burgundy bruiser."

"You up to it?"

"Of course. I was only drugged and buried alive. Don't fuss, dear."

She snorted a laugh and slapped the keys into my hand. "Asshole."

"What does a guy need to do to get some sympathy around here?"

I eased myself behind the wheel and fired up the big old growler. Dehan climbed in beside me. I put it in first and pulled away, headed east toward FDR Drive. We drove in silence for a few minutes and finally she said, "We *are* going to need a few days, Stone." I nodded, and she went on. "It was traumatic for me. I really thought you were dead. I can't imagine what it was like for you."

"Hell."

"It must have been."

"I'll need breakfast in bed for the next week at least. Maybe two."

"Don't joke about it, Stone. You'll probably have PTSD. You need to take this seriously."

"I will." I grinned at her. "I will add it to the list of things I need counseling for."

"You're a jerk, Stone. I'm being serious."

"I know you are. So am I. You know what still gives me nightmares? When I found you in that lockup, inhaling gas. I still get flashbacks from that. And when you were abducted in the Westchester Angel case.[1] I really thought you were dead then. Those are the events that have traumatized me, Dehan."

She exhaled through her teeth and turned away. "You big, old . . ."

---

1. See *To Kill Upon a Kiss.*

She was quiet for a while then, blinking a lot until she finally wiped her eyes on her sleeve, pulled out a handkerchief, and blew her nose. When she spoke, she sounded like she had a cold.

"Well, even if you don't get counseling, I think we need some time. You know, to kind of process this and . . . you know what I mean."

"Back at the dawn of time, when I was young, before we had counselors and everything had an acronym, we didn't process things. We took time to get over them. Sometimes that involved getting drunk, other times it involved lying on a beach and sunbathing a lot. Or both. For girls it also involved crying, because, back then, guys didn't cry, but we would stare at the horizon a lot, and throw stones into the sea. Is that the kind of thing you had in mind?"

She giggled wetly and started crying again. Then she nodded. "Uh-huh."

"Sounds good to me, Dehan. I could use some of that."

She sniffed and blinked at the road for a bit. Then she frowned. "Where are you going, Stone? We don't need to go to the station. We're going home."

"Yeah, I just need to take a small detour on the way."

We were on the Bruckner Expressway, and I peeled off to join the boulevard at White Plains Road. Dehan's face had become rigid. At the bridge, I turned left and crossed over the expressway. Then I turned left into Watson Avenue. Her jaw dropped and she turned to look at me.

"Son of a bitch!" she said.

I raised an eyebrow at her. "You hadn't worked it out?"

"Last night, but this whole thing with Helena . . . I thought I was wrong. What was that all about?"

"It had been nagging at my mind since I glanced at the list of students. I didn't know. I was drugged and groggy and my memory was patchy. It had to be explored. I wasn't sure of anything."

We came to St. Lawrence Avenue and turned in. There I stopped outside the white clapboard house and climbed out.

Peter Heseltine opened the door and smiled at us in some surprise.

"Detectives! What can I do for you?"

"We just want a few minutes of your time."

"Well, of course. Come in. You're lucky to find me here, I would normally be at work."

I shrugged. "We were passing by. It was on the off chance."

"Sure."

He led us into a comfortable living room on the ground floor overlooking the front yard. The furnishings were good, but old, and had a feminine quality to them. "I had assumed, when we dropped you off, that you had an apartment upstairs."

"Oh, no, I inherited the house from my mom. I've never really done anything with it. Please, sit. Coffee?"

I shook my head, and we sat. He sat too, on the sofa. I gave him an expressionless stare and said, "Is Helena Magnusson here?"

He went white. "Of course not! Why would she be?"

I gave another shrug. "She's not at her house. I know you have a big crush on her. I thought she might be here."

"Good Lord! A crush? Me? Whatever gave you that idea?"

"Well, you were pretty complimentary about her in the car. You described her as 'superbly, elegantly European.' You also avoided talking about her and dodged Detective Dehan's question about how well you knew her. So I put it all together and decided you had a crush on her."

He laughed. "Forgive me for saying so, Detective, but I think you have put one and one together and made five. I did not have a crush on Helena."

I nodded. "No, I have understated the case. You didn't have a crush. You were insanely in love with her."

His eyebrows rose up high on his forehead. "Based on my describing her as elegantly European?"

"That and the fact that you joined her creative writing classes."

He stared at me for a long time. His mouth was working but nothing was coming out. Finally he said, "That's hardly . . ."

"It would be nothing at all if you had told us about it from the start. But the fact that you never mentioned it is odd to the point of being highly incriminating. You must have gone there the night she received the package with her husband's head in it. You must have known all her pupils in the class. You must have known Lenny dos Santos. You might have been a key witness, and yet you never said a word. You didn't tell the original investigators, and you didn't tell us during that long rant you had while you were in my car. In fact, all you did do during that rant was point the finger at Penelope Peach."

"You're grasping at straws, Detective."

"Am I? How about if I tell you that I recognized you?"

"What?"

"You have very short eyelashes. Helena has quite long ones. Your eyes are blue; hers are a deep brown. You screwed up your doses of whatever it was you were feeding me, Peter. What was it, ketamine? I'm a big man. You needed a higher dose. Look at me, I am up and about just a few hours later! I told you at the time I recognized you, and you thought I had fallen for your dumb trick and recognized Helena. But I hadn't, I had recognized you."

"That's absurd. I have no idea what you're talking about."

"I recognized you, Peter!"

"That's not possible!"

"Why not?"

"Because . . . Because I wasn't there!"

"Where?"

"Wherever it was that you thought you recognized me!"

"In your cellar."

He swallowed hard. I waited. He swallowed again.

"How about it, Peter? Want to show me your cellar, and prove beyond any doubt that I was never there and it wasn't you?"

"You're out of your mind. Go and get a court order if you think you can. And now I want you out of my house!"

I stood. "Peter Heseltine, I am placing you under arrest for the murder of Jack Connors, the murder of Ebba, Helena's maidservant, the kidnapping and attempted murder of Detective John Stone, and the kidnapping and attempted murder of Helena Magnusson."

He screamed. He screamed like a cornered animal, a rat or a ferret, and he sprang at me with his fingers hooked like claws. Smashing my fist into his face was one of the most satisfying moments of my life. His legs turned to spaghetti, and he dropped to the floor with a *whoomph!*

EPILOGUE

HELENA WAS STILL ALIVE, THOUGH SHE HAD BEEN TIED to the same table where I had been tied, and the cheese cutter was poised to sever her head at any time. She was taken away in an ambulance, and Deputy Inspector John Newman assured us, with some enthusiasm, that he would happily take her statement himself, in person.

After that, and after we had had a word with Joe, who was heading up the crime scene team, Dehan drove us home, set me up in a deck chair, gave me a large glass of Bushmills, and set about lighting the charcoal in the barbeque. I watched her do it with an idiot grin on my face and listened to the birds preparing for bed in the trees.

"You have to tell me, Stone, when did you realize it was Peter?"

I sighed and thought about it.

"Too late. He was right there on her list of pupils, and neither of us registered it until it was too late. He was always there in my mind, like a dull toothache. He was so insignificant, so nondescript, yet so eager to discredit Jack Connors and point the finger at Penelope."

I leaned my head back and closed my eyes.

"It was a kind of drip, drip. I realized from the start that Jack had not been the real target. It had been Helena. There had been an attempt to communicate something to her. Of course it might have been Penelope telling her, 'If I can't have him, neither can you!' But as it turned out, Penelope *did* have him, and it was Helena who had lost him. So it made no sense for her to kill him.

"Then there were Grant, Lenny, and Alornerk. They all had possible motives to kill Jack, but not to send *that* message to Helena. Grant's motive for killing Jack would have been so that he could have Penelope for himself. So Helena would have been of absolutely no interest to him. He would be more likely to keep the head as a trophy than send it to her.

"Again, Lenny would have had no reason to send her Jack's head. If he had, what would the message have been? It was not a gesture, or a statement, that would mean anything to Lenny.

"As for Alornerk, the statement might have had more meaning to his mind, but the act of killing Jack was a senseless one for him. They remained friends, but he made no attempt to get back together with her, and besides, as we later found out, he was in fact in bed with her at the time that Jack was killed, so his loss was not so great as to drive him to murder. And in the circumstances, sending her Jack's head would have been pretty senseless if they had just been in bed together.

"It began to seem that the most compelling theory was that Helena had done it herself, and your argument that sending herself the head provided a powerful defense on top of a double alibi was pretty persuasive. But there were problems. If she had killed him herself, it meant that Alornerk was in it with her, providing her with not one, but two false alibis: that they had gone to lunch with fictitious European friends *and* that they had been in bed together. So, if he was going to stick to the second alibi, why blow the first? Why tell us the European friends were fake if he was then going to tell us he was in bed with her?

"Plus, every description of her supposed accomplice said he was average height and nondescript. Alornerk was tall and thin and had a face like an upside-down pear. So Alornerk was *not* her accomplice, which meant the second alibi was true.

"And all the while I had this nagging in my mind. We kept saying it, remember? We have to take another look at the list of pupils. I had this nagging that said there was somebody manipulating the situation, making us see what he wanted us to see. It began to dawn on me when I left the station and went to see Penelope. Peter's background was in computer graphics and special effects. The gesture of the head in the cool box inside a UPS package had all the hallmarks of a man trained in special effects.

"I drove past his place on the way to Penelope's and saw that he was at home—or at least somebody was—and it registered in my mind that his house was very close to Underhill Community Center. But what hadn't registered yet was that I had seen his name on the list of pupils at her class. And the one thing that stopped him being a prime suspect was that he had no real connection with her.

"Then it hit me in the hospital. You used the word 'disciples' and it registered. His name. I saw it clear as day in my mind. Peter Heseltine, and I knew that he had let me go, not to redeem himself, but because he was placing Helena firmly in the frame because he planned to kill her."

"That's what I don't get."

I opened my eyes.

She had turned to look at me. "Why did he suddenly decide to kill her?"

"I can only guess. He was a deeply inhibited young man who had obviously developed an obsession with her on the occasions she used to go into the office and charm their pants off. His obsession grew, partly because he had to endure Jack daily flaunting his affair with Penelope, and partly when he plucked up the courage to join her class.

"He was so nondescript and so invisible that she didn't even notice he was the same guy from her husband's office, but he was in denial about that. We'll know for sure when we interrogate him, but two gets you twenty he developed a fantasy in which she was secretly falling in love with him, and he was going to save her. Just like we said about Lenny, only in this case it was Peter sending her 'messages' through his stories, and taking her words of *literary* encouragement as words of encouragement in his fantasy. His stories were probably littered with phrases and situations about him and her, which she never saw for what they were. But all she had to do was scrawl 'keep trying' or 'a very moving piece of work' in the margin for him to believe that she was responding to his secret, coded messages and urging him on.

"Yet, after he had killed Jack and sent her the very powerful message, 'I have set you free,' she disappeared from his life. She never went back to class, and she never returned to the office. His dream came crashing down overnight. And he was far too emotionally crippled and inhibited ever to go to her house to talk to her in person. He must have been devastated."

She nodded and cracked open a bottle of beer. "Then we came along, saying we had reopened the case, and he was suddenly looking at going to prison for the rest of his life for nothing. He had killed his boss for her, and she had just turned her back on him and walked away. His betrayed love must have turned very quickly to hatred and vengeance."

"Exactly."

She went indoors and came out after a while with a plate of steaks and started dousing them with oil and pepper. After a moment, she stopped and frowned.

"But what about the decapitated bodies that were found around Madison?"

"Again, we'll have to confirm it in interrogation, but he was at pains to deflect suspicion in many directions, and it seemed to me that the killer had gone to some lengths to make it look like the possible work of a serial killer. So I wondered if he had killed again afterwards." I paused, frowning at the sky, just beginning to turn copper and pink overhead. "In fact, if I am honest, Dehan, what I really wondered was whether the killer wasn't actually a homicidal psychopath, using his obsession with Helena as an excuse to kill, who had then got a taste for it. What struck me was that the other two bodies had not had their heads dispatched anywhere by UPS. And notice that he never dismantled his cheese cutter."

"Jesus, Stone." She shook her head. "That would never have occurred to me."

"It didn't really occur to me, Dehan. It was just one possible ramification. If the killer wanted us to believe he or she was a psychotic killer, he might kill again using a similar MO."

"But, secretly, it was because he was enjoying it."

I shrugged. "I don't think anyone kills in such an elaborate, inventive manner unless they are actually enjoying it."

She took a pull on her beer and turned to toss the steaks on the barbeque. They sizzled, and tall flames leapt from the coals and licked and seared the meat. The smell of burning aromatic herbs and barbecued meat wafted on the evening air.

I smiled. I watched her in silence, her slim legs and her elegant waist, and her long, black hair tied into a loose knot behind her neck, and felt myself healing inside.

"I love you," I said.

She turned, surprised, and smiled, and her eyes shone.

Don't miss THE FALL MOON. The riveting sequel in the Dead Cold Mystery series.

Scan the QR code below to purchase THE FALL MOON.

Or go to: righthouse.com/the-fall-moon

NOTE: flip to the very end to read an exclusive sneak peak...

DON'T MISS ANYTHING!

If you want to stay up to date on all new releases in this series, with this author, or with any of our new deals, you can do so by joining our newsletters below.

In addition, you will immediately gain access to our entire *Right House VIP Library,* which includes many riveting Mystery and Thriller novels for your enjoyment!

righthouse.com/email

(Easy to unsubscribe. No spam. Ever.)

ALSO BY BLAKE BANNER

Up to date books can be found at:
www.righthouse.com/blake-banner

ROGUE THRILLERS
Gates of Hell (Book 1)
Hell's Fury (Book 2)

ALEX MASON THRILLERS
Odin (Book 1)
Ice Cold Spy (Book 2)
Mason's Law (Book 3)
Assets and Liabilities (Book 4)
Russian Roulette (Book 5)
Executive Order (Book 6)
Dead Man Talking (Book 7)
All The King's Men (Book 8)
Flashpoint (Book 9)
Brotherhood of the Goat (Book 10)
Dead Hot (Book 11)
Blood on Megiddo (Book 12)
Son of Hell (Book 13)

HARRY BAUER THRILLER SERIES
Dead of Night (Book 1)
Dying Breath (Book 2)
The Einstaat Brief (Book 3)
Quantum Kill (Book 4)
Immortal Hate (Book 5)
The Silent Blade (Book 6)
LA: Wild Justice (Book 7)

Breath of Hell (Book 8)
Invisible Evil (Book 9)
The Shadow of Ukupacha (Book 10)
Sweet Razor Cut (Book 11)
Blood of the Innocent (Book 12)
Blood on Balthazar (Book 13)
Simple Kill (Book 14)
Riding The Devil (Book 15)
The Unavenged (Book 16)
The Devil's Vengeance (Book 17)
Bloody Retribution (Book 18)
Rogue Kill (Book 19)
Blood for Blood (Book 20)

DEAD COLD MYSTERY SERIES
An Ace and a Pair (Book 1)
Two Bare Arms (Book 2)
Garden of the Damned (Book 3)
Let Us Prey (Book 4)
The Sins of the Father (Book 5)
Strange and Sinister Path (Book 6)
The Heart to Kill (Book 7)
Unnatural Murder (Book 8)
Fire from Heaven (Book 9)
To Kill Upon A Kiss (Book 10)
Murder Most Scottish (Book 11)
The Butcher of Whitechapel (Book 12)
Little Dead Riding Hood (Book 13)
Trick or Treat (Book 14)
Blood Into Wine (Book 15)
Jack In The Box (Book 16)
The Fall Moon (Book 17)
Blood In Babylon (Book 18)
Death In Dexter (Book 19)
Mustang Sally (Book 20)

ABOUT US

Right House is an independent publisher created by authors for readers. We specialize in Action, Thriller, Mystery, and Crime novels.

If you enjoyed this novel, then there is a good chance you will like what else we have to offer! Please stay up to date by using any of the links below.

Join our mailing lists to stay up to date -->
righthouse.com/email
Visit our website --> righthouse.com
Contact us --> contact@righthouse.com

 facebook.com/righthousebooks

 x.com/righthousebooks

 instagram.com/righthousebooks

EXCLUSIVE SNEAK PEAK OF...

THE FALL MOON

CHAPTER 1

"You remember the Redfern case?"

Dehan spoke to the bacon on her plate as she cut into it, frowning. I leaned back comfortably, holding my coffee cup halfway to my mouth.

"Sure, it was Bob Lindsey's case just before he got shot." I scratched my chin. "Six, seven years ago? Couple killed in their home on Ellis Avenue, few doors down from the Glory of Christ church, as I recall. Daughter disappeared, presumed killed too. Bobby died. The shooting was unrelated to the case. Case went cold." I sipped my coffee. Outside, birds were singing in the warm, summer Sunday morning. "You want to look at that case?"

She shrugged and pulled a face at the same time. "I was always curious." She eyed me while she wiped her mouth with her napkin. "I have a feeling about that case, Stone. It was seven years ago this fall . . ." She tapped her temple with her finger. "And it's still up here. I don't know why we never looked at it." She took the same finger and wagged it at me. "There is more to that case than meets the eye, and you knew it at the time. I could see it, writ large on your ugly face."

"Thanks."

"Your face isn't ugly. Don't get sensitive. You know what I'm saying."

"Yeah, it caught a lot of people's attention at the time. But what can I tell you? It wasn't my case. They hit a dead end . . ."

"He got shot."

"That didn't help. What's your point, Dehan?"

She laid her knife and fork across her plate, picked up her cup, and frowned into her coffee.

"There was more to that case than that couple getting stabbed to death. I was interested at the time, but I was a rookie. I wish I'd been your partner back then. We should have taken the case. There were threads that were never followed. I knew you were thinking back then that the case should never have gone cold."

"How could you know that?"

She smiled. "I was aware of you."

"Really? Back then?"

"Sure, you were this wiseass, smart-ass with a bad attitude who had a kick-ass record for solving hard cases."

"So it was all about the ass?"

"You know it."

I shrugged and then followed up with a nod. "It's true, I did think that at the time. Bobby's partner . . ." I thought for a moment. "Sanchez. He kind of sat on it for a while. Then it went cold. I had cases of my own . . ."

"You know what?" She frowned. "There were aspects to the case I often thought could have made it a federal case."

I was surprised. I thought back, trying to remember. It had been six years ago and the details were hazy. "I'm not sure, Dehan. I can't think of anything offhand that would take it out of the purview of the NYPD and bring it within the jurisdiction of the bureau . . . Talk me through."

She poured herself more coffee. I held out my cup and she refilled mine too. Then she sat back, holding her cup in both hands, her eyes became abstracted, and she started to recite from memory.

"Karl and Christen Redfern, 2163 Ellis Avenue, first-floor apartment. Occupied by them and their daughter, Amy. Sometime between the night of Saturday the twenty-second and the small hours of Sunday the twenty-third of September, 2012, somebody entered their apartment and killed Karl and Christen. His body was found in the kitchen. He had been stabbed in the right kidney, once, with a long, broad, sharp blade, probably a kitchen knife. He was then stabbed in the heart, through the fourth and fifth intercostals. However, bleeding from the kidney had been profuse, whereas he had bled little from the heart, suggesting the wound to the heart was perimortem.

"Christen was killed in their bed while she was sleeping. There were between fifteen and twenty stab wounds to the heart. It was hard to be precise because the area was so damaged and badly lacerated, the ribs themselves had been fractured and broken. Bruising, pre-, peri-, and postmortem, was extensive. She also had bruising to the face, and other parts of her body, suggesting the attack went on some time while she was dying, and after she was dead.

"Amy Redfern was not found at the house, or anywhere else. No trace of her has ever been found."

She sipped her coffee and set down her cup with care, like she was centering her ideas on the tabletop. She went on:

"Of note are the fact that the prints found at the scene were predominantly Karl's and Christen's, Amy's, and her boyfriend, Charlie's. That is to be expected, but there were no prints that were attributable to a killer on the kitchen knives, the surfaces, or the victims themselves.

"One large kitchen knife was found in the drying rack by the sink. There were no traces of blood or fingerprints on it. Normally, when crockery or cutlery is washed, some prints are found, but this knife had been polished clean. The blade was consistent with the weapon used to kill both of the Redferns and was probably the murder weapon."

I grunted. "Do I remember correctly that the lock had been

very crudely forced? Hadn't the wood been hacked away from the latch with some kind of blade, like a screwdriver?"

She nodded. "That's right. And, final point of interest, both Karl and Christen had cannabis, coke, and alcohol in their systems."

I gazed out the window, across the living room, wondering why we couldn't spend Sunday morning like normal people, going to the park, or driving out to the country. But the case was coming back to me, and I had to admit, it was interesting, and had intrigued me at the time. Absently, I said, "No motive ever became apparent either, did it?"

"Nope."

She stood and walked over to the window I'd been looking out of and stood with her hands in the back pockets of her jeans, gazing at the street. After a moment, she turned and sat on the sill.

"There was no cash found in the house, which may or may not be significant. According to neighbors, they struggled to get by and spent whatever disposable income they had on booze and drugs, mainly weed." She shrugged. "If I were going to burglarize a house, I would not have chosen theirs. You wouldn't need to go very far to find a better candidate."

I watched her lean down and grab her bag from beside the sofa. From it she pulled a case file, gave me a guilty grin, and brought it to the breakfast table. I sighed and reached for it as she handed it to me.

"Dehan, it's Sunday. The day even God kicked back and put his feet up."

"I know, Stone, but I started rereading it and it got under my skin. What happened to that girl? You know what I mean. I know you do."

I opened the file and she lifted out the crime scene photos till she found the photographs of the two bodies, his in the kitchen, slumped on the floor in a dark pool of blood, and hers facedown on the bed. We both studied them for a minute. Then I smiled to myself because I knew she was thinking the same as me.

"What struck me back then was that he was attacked initially from behind, and though it wasn't expert, it was efficient: a single, disabling stab to the kidney, and as he turned and collapsed, another to the heart."

She looked at me and nodded. "I know . . ."

I went on, "But the attack on Christen was totally different. It's savage and frenzied, delivered with enough force to break bone . . ."

She was nodding as I spoke. "So you're thinking that Christen was the actual target. He got Karl out of the way, went into the bedroom, and let rip."

I nodded. "Yeah, it's possible, isn't it? There can't be much doubt that she was the focus of real rage, and he wasn't."

She scratched her head, then tied up her hair. She looked in her cup, put it down, and glanced out the window. I watched her do all that, frowning, and she grinned at me.

"You want to go see the scene?" I raised a skeptical eyebrow and questioned her with it. She said, "The landlord wants to sell it, so he's keeping it vacant. I called him. I told him we probably wouldn't come today, being Sunday an' all, but that, you know . . . we might."

I stared at her a moment.

She went on, "He said that would be fine, so long as we don't scare away potential buyers . . . Are you mad?"

"No. I love examining crime scenes on my days off. It makes such a change from what I do the rest of the week."

"You're mad."

"No! No, really. It's obviously got under your skin, so let's go scratch that itch."

I stood, and she stared at me, then smiled. "See? That's why I married you out of four billion men."

"Flattery, Dehan, will get you exactly . . ."

"Everywhere with you. Everywhere . . ."

"Exactly. Everywhere. Let's go."

I pulled on my jacket and gathered together keys and phone.

It was a warm, quiet Sunday. The birds were busy in the plane trees doing whatever it is that birds do when they won't stop chattering. I tossed Dehan the keys to my old, burgundy Jaguar Mark II and made my way to the passenger door.

"Least you can do is drive me, as you're making me work on my day off."

She caught them left-handed without looking and unlocked the car. "Quit griping, I'll make it up to you."

I climbed in and slammed the door. "Damn right you will. Exactly what did you have in mind?"

She fired up the old bruiser and sniggered. "I'll buy you a new pair of slippers, and a pipe."

I scowled at her. "I don't wear slippers, Dehan, and I don't smoke a pipe."

She pulled out and accelerated toward Morris Park Avenue. "And I'll get you a comfy old cardigan to go with them."

"Take a hike. This is the thanks I get: mockery!"

She'd started laughing. "Then you can sit Sunday mornings and watch the sports and get mad at the news."

It was a fifteen-minute drive from Haight Avenue to Ellis Avenue, but it was Sunday, the roads were empty, and Dehan was driving, so we did it in ten. All the way she sniggered, and I made a careful study of the shop fronts.

2163 Ellis Avenue was a slightly dilapidated, rust-colored clapboard house with nice big bay windows on the ground floor and the upper floor. It also had a nice porch with five stone steps leading down to the sidewalk and a white wrought iron railing that looked as though it had recently been painted. A large sign had been attached to those railings, advertising the house for sale.

We climbed the steps to where a small, brown awning protected the front door from rain and sun and studied the two mailboxes and the two bells on the entry-phone. Both bells had a faded, misted window where you could put a card with your name on it. They were both empty. Dehan had phoned the landlord from the car to let him know we were coming. Now she pressed the bottom bell and a tired voice said, "Yeah . . ." like he'd figured we thought life was barely worth living, and he was agreeing with us.

"Good morning, sir, this is Detective Dehan of the NYPD. I called about ten minutes ago . . ."

"Yuh . . ." He made it sound like it was a shame she called about ten minutes ago, but there wasn't much he could do about it. The door buzzed. I pushed it open and stood back for Dehan to go ahead, then followed her into a handsome, well-proportioned hall with an ugly, beige carpet and a broad, mahogany staircase climbing the left-hand wall. On the right, there was a large door which opened, as the street door closed, to reveal a small man in big brown pants and a big colorless cardigan. His face looked as tired as his voice had sounded. We showed him our badges. Dehan spoke.

"Mr. Bernstein? I am Detective Dehan. This is my partner, Detective Stone."

He looked at us curiously, then his eyes smiled.

"Sure. I know. Come in." It was all said with the kind of resignation that you buy into because they persuade you it's a virtue. By the time you realize it's not, it's too late, because you've already resigned yourself to it. He walked away from us into a large, bright room that ran the full length of the building. He spoke as he walked, in small, tired steps.

"It was my sister's house. She died. Everybody dies. Sooner or later. But it's still a surprise when they do." After a moment, he added, "I never thought she would ever die."

On the right as we stepped in was the bay window. Ahead there was an open fireplace with a black, marble hearth. Against the opposite wall there was an old, leather sofa that had once been expensive, before it was donated, and two armchairs that hadn't. They all sat around an unattractive coffee table that was pretending to be pine but failing to convince.

On the left, the area that had once been a dining room was now a kitchen-diner, with a long, fake mahogany table running sideways across the room. In the far wall, there were two doors which I figured were the bedrooms. Mr. Bernstein had his ass against the dining table and was watching us.

I said, "You remember the Redferns?"

"Oh, yes. They died too, but for different reasons. My sister died of old age. She was very old." He shrugged in a way that suggested he found a certain pleasure in the self-evident, and added, "Old enough to die."

I asked, "What were they like?"

"Sad. The daughter was sweet, a bit neurotic. He used to beat them, of course. I guess enough of that could make you neurotic, right? They drank a lot. But one tries not to pry. Would you like me to leave while you do your *Monk* thing?" He smiled and held out his hands in front of him as though he was lining up a shot for a camera.

Dehan smiled and nodded. "We'd appreciate that."

"I'll be down the road. You have my number."

The door closed behind him, and a moment later, the sound from the street swelled a second before being cut off when that door was closed too.

CHAPTER 2

WE STARED AT EACH OTHER A MOMENT, NOT AWARE that we were staring, but somehow sharing our thoughts. I pointed at the kitchen. "You're Karl."

She nodded and went over to the sink, talking over her shoulder. "He was making coffee, right?"

I went to the door of the apartment. "Yeah, and this is one of the things that always unsettled me. If you're in the kitchen, making coffee, how come you don't hear me peeling the wood away from the latch?"

She thought about it for a moment. "There are two possible answers to that, and they might both apply. First, both Karl and Christen are stoned out of their minds. So while our killer was cutting through the wood, Karl might well have been stood here watching the kettle boil, communing with the fairies and giggling to himself."

I gave my head a little twitch and asked, "Or?"

"Or Karl might have been as unconscious as Christen when the killer came in. He needed to pee, most likely got hungry and thirsty—you know how it is . . ."

"No."

"Maybe the breaking of the latch was what woke him and he didn't realize it. So he gets up *after* the killer broke in."

I made the face of a person who is not satisfied. "Okay, so you're in the bedroom. Go in the bedroom . . ."

"Which one? I don't remember."

"Have a look."

She peered through both doors and turned to face me. "Okay, that one on the left is Amy's."

I nodded.

"This one on the right is bigger and has the en suite."

I waved her through the door and I called out to her as I went through the motions of busting the latch.

"Okay, so I break in, meanwhile you fall out of bed, stagger to the toilet. I hear you moving about, I hear you flush, so I hide . . . where?"

I looked about. She appeared in the bedroom doorway. I glanced at her and went on. "I guess I flatten myself in the corner, beyond the dining table. The light switch is over in the kitchen, so he hasn't switched it on yet and it's still dark. Now you move to the kitchen . . ."

She crossed the floor into the kitchen and began to move around like she was making coffee. I moved around the dining table and crept up behind her, stopped, and sighed noisily.

"See? There are too many problems with this theory, but the big one right now is this." She turned to look at me and she was nodding, like she already knew what I was going to say. I went on anyway. "Did you notice in the crime scene photos where the block with the kitchen knives was?"

She pointed at the surface behind her. "The obvious place, by the cooker."

"So to get the kitchen knife to kill you with, I have to go *past* you without being seen, and then come *back* behind you, to stab you in the kidney."

She shrugged one shoulder. "It's possible the knife was not in the block. It may have been on the table."

I shook my head. "Even so, that's just part of it; what nagged at me from the start was, *I already have a weapon.* I just used it to hack away the lock. Why do I wait for you to get all the way across to the kitchen, get a mug, get the instant coffee from the cupboard, spoon it into the mug, switch on the kettle, *and only then* grab the knife and stab you in the back—all that instead of stabbing you right from the start with the tool I used on the door? What have I been doing all this time?"

We stared at each other for a moment. "After that point it works fine," I said. "You're about to pour the water onto the coffee, I come up behind you, stab you once in the kidney, you turn as you go down and I stab you once in the heart. But how and *for what purpose* I got hold of the kitchen knife is not clear. That period from entry to stabbing, that does not satisfy me at all."

She nodded. "I agree." She mimed killing Karl, stabbing him in the heart on the kitchen floor, then looked over at the bedroom. "So at that point, he moves quickly to the bedroom door. There is enough light from the kitchen for him to see that Christen is lying on the bed. We don't know if she was facedown or not to begin with. She took a hell of a beating. But she winds up facedown and that's when he goes into his frenzied attack with the knife. Then he returns to the kitchen, thoroughly washes the knife, leaves it in the rack, and goes."

"But that brings us to the other problem."

"Amy."

I nodded. "Amy."

"The crime scene report said the room was in a mess . . ."

"The room *was* in a mess," I said. "But it didn't look as though it had been turned over or ransacked. It just looked like the room of a young woman who doesn't clean up often. It was like her parents' room." I shrugged. "The sheets on the bed were dirty, there were dirty clothes on the floor, dirty underwear. There was a bowl of cereal under the bed that had gone moldy, an ashtray on the bedside table that was brimming over. A lot of the butts were joints. There was, apparently at least, nothing essential missing, other than her cell and her purse."

She pulled out a chair, sat, and rested her elbows on the table. "So either she wasn't here when the killing happened, or she was here and left with the killer."

"Both of those scenarios beg questions." I raised my thumb as number one. "If she wasn't here when the killing happened, why didn't she come back at some stage? Her closet was full of clothes, all her books, her iPod; as far as they could tell at the time, everything she possessed except her phone and her purse were in her room. And in six years she never showed up, never phoned, never contacted anybody . . ."

Dehan spread her hands. "But likewise, if she left with the killer, was it voluntary or involuntary? The very fact that she never took any of her stuff suggests she hadn't planned for it and she wasn't leaving of her own free will, right?"

I nodded. "Yeah, it does."

"So, what I am thinking, Stone, is that he has abducted her, and he has either kept her against her will or, more likely, he has killed her and dumped her body somewhere."

I shoved my hands in my pockets and moved across the room toward the two big windows. An afternoon breeze shifted the dappled shade on the blacktop. A hint of the approaching fall tinged the light with copper. I spoke aloud, staring out through the glass at the street. "Whatever it was, that was one messed-up motive. The focus of his attack is the mother. He beats her, then stabs her fifteen or twenty times, all in the heart. That's *a lot of focus*, all on her heart, and then he takes the daughter, without a struggle." I turned. "He lets her take her cell and her purse, and then he kills her. I have a lot of trouble understanding what is motivating him."

Her form was slightly hazy in the half-light, staring down at the tabletop. "I know," she said. "I agree. But that's what it looks like he did, right? So what that means is that there are bits missing from the picture. There is something that connects the mother, the daughter, and the killer in a way that makes sense of the killer's rage and his decision to abduct Amy."

"You've decided she was abducted?"

"That's putting it a bit strong, but I am pretty sure of it. *I'm* having trouble making sense of any other explanation. If she'd run, she would have called for help, or called the cops. If he'd killed her here, there'd have been a body, or blood, or signs of a struggle . . ."

"And you think you know what this missing piece is?"

She sighed, made a doubtful face, and got to her feet. "Maybe. Let's say I have a hunch that I know the kind of area where we might find it. You done here?"

I nodded.

"Good. C'mon, I'll buy you an ice cream in Central Park."

"In Central Park . . ."

"Sure. It's Sunday. We go to the park. Live a little." She went and opened the door, holding it for me. "See, that's the problem with you, Stone. It's always work, work, work. My father would have told you: 'Son, take a rest on the Sabbath.' He was a wise man."

I sighed, shook my head, and followed her out to the car.

We drove twenty-five minutes to Manhattan. All the way, she talked about everything you could possibly imagine talking about in the short space of twenty-five minutes, while I thought about the crossword I'd been planning to do, drinking lemonade in the backyard.

We dropped the car near the corner of East 106th and crossed 5th Avenue at a slow lope. We found the Conservatory Garden gate and went in among the lawns and the trees around the Harlem Meer. There, we stopped at the kiosk. I told her I didn't want an ice cream and she ordered two vanilla cones, then slapped me on the chest with the back of her hand. "C'mon, loosen up. Have some fun. When was the last time you had an ice cream, *pendejo*?"

I smiled and after a moment asked her, "Do you know what *pendejo* means, Dehan?"

"What do you think?" She put money on the counter, took the two cones, and handed one to me. She started licking as we started to walk. "My mother was Mexican. All her family are Mexican. Of course I know what it means. It means asshole, idiot, dickwad. It's a serious insult in Mexico, but the way I use it, it's not. It's like, 'Hey, asshole,' 'Hey, *pendejo*.' It's like a term of endearment."

I shifted my fingers to avoid the drips of melting cream. "It means pubic hair."

She raised an eyebrow at me.

I went on. "You call somebody a *pendejo* and you're calling them a pubic hair. So what's this hunch you have?"

She switched eyebrows, sighed, and returned to her cone. "Jeez . . . So, all that time ago, when I was a rookie, I never got the chance to talk to you about the case. It wasn't my case, you were kind of this senior, forbidding guy who was always busy; plus, now you've mellowed a bit, but back then you had this real bad attitude. And I was just . . . you know . . . a rookie. Then, by the time I'd screwed up enough courage, Bob got shot, Sanchez took over and sat on the case. It went cold . . . So, I never got to discuss it with you and I don't know if you were aware of it."

"Aware of what?"

We were following the path along the water, and I was wondering if I could drop the cone in and make it look like an accident.

"Six, almost seven months before Karl and Christen were killed, sometime in March, he was badly beaten and put in hospital."

I stopped and stared down at her, aware that she had said something important but not aware why. "By whom?"

She grinned and started walking again. "Whom? It kills me when you say that. I always wanted a partner who said things like 'whom' and quoted Conan Doyle. 'Eliminate the impossible, Dehan . . .'"

I caught up with her. "Dehan! What has got into you today? Who beat him up?"

She shrugged, still grinning. "He refused to testify, said he didn't see who it was, but it seemed like a big coincidence, you know what I mean?"

"Wait a minute, slow down." I stopped again. My hand was covered in melted cream and I switched the cone to my other hand so I could lick my finger. "How did you find out about this . . .?"

"What can I tell you? I liked the case. I was curious. You going to eat that?"

"No."

"Why didn't you just say?" She took it from me and started licking it. "We had a stabbed homeless guy, and a son of a bitch who beat his wife to death." I crouched down to wet my finger in the meer. She went on talking. "I'm not saying they weren't important. Everybody's life is important, I get that. But they weren't exactly sudoku either. Plus, my partner was a real asshole. I'm not a feminist, but every damn word out of his mouth was about my ass or my boobs."

I stood and we started walking again.

"So I took an interest in the Redfern case and I started snooping around. I'm good at snooping around. You know? Looking at the angles . . . ?" She did a little duck and dive and stuffed the last of my cone in her mouth. "So I figured maybe I should find out a little about Karl and Christen. Maybe it was a ghost from their past that came and bit them in the ass."

I nodded. "Yeah, I had wondered that."

"Yeah, I figured. Then Bob got shot, and Captain Peralta didn't want to know when I asked her if I could take the case." She shrugged. "So I put the word out with a couple of informants. I wanted to know who put Karl Redfern in hospital."

"And?"

She stopped and narrowed her eyes at me, poked me gently on the chest with her finger. "See? Like me, you think it's going to be a big revelation, open up the case." She shook her head and looked past me at where the midday sun was sparkling on the meer. "Adolfo Davila and Mateo Bonilla, from the Bronx. Both members of the Chupacabras."

I frowned. "Did you talk to them?"

She shook her head, still gazing out at the coppery water. "Both dead."

"Both dead . . . ?"

She thrust her hands in her pockets, hunched her shoulders, and turned slowly on her heel to start walking again. "You're going to ask me how and when."

I fell into step. "Mm-hm . . ."

"They were shot point-blank down by the fish market on Hunts Point. Nine-millimeter hollow points. One each to the chest, then one each to the head when they were down."

"An execution."

She stopped and wagged a finger at me. "An execution, but note, not execution *style*." She shook her head. "Every badass kid from a 'hood' all across the U.S.A. who watches TV can't wait to get out on the streets with his new nine-millimeter Taurus and kill some poor schmuck 'execution style.'" She held out her hands like she was holding a gun and snarled, "Git on yo' knees, mother focker! *Bam! Execution style!*" She started walking again. "But this wasn't execution *style*. This was . . . *efficient*. They didn't see it coming. *Bam! Bam!* One each in the chest. Then he confirmed the kill. No waste of time, no waste of ammo. No evidence."

"Shells? Slugs?"

"The four slugs. No shells."

"When?"

"The night of the twenty-sixth to the twenty-seventh of August, 2012."

"Less than a month before Karl and Christen."

"And neither Karl nor Christen owned a gun."

I crossed the path on slow feet and sat on the bench that runs along the gardens opposite the lake. She came and sat next to me. I had my elbows on my knees, but she was leaning back with the ankle of her right leg on her left knee.

"And what you're trying to do is show that these four murders are connected, and tie them to the Chupacabras."

She sat forward and leaned gently against me. "Let's take it one step at a time, partner. I am not *trying to show* that they are connected. They are connected, because the guys who got killed at the fish market are the same guys who put Karl in hospital; that right there is a connection. What I want to show is that these are parts of the same crime. There are other connections, some are more obvious, others are more subtle."

I frowned at her. "You been working on this on your own, without telling me?"

"Not exactly, but I have looked at it from time to time."

"Huh . . . Okay, tell me the more obvious connections."

"Drugs."

"Karl was a user, mainly weed . . ."

"Yeah, but also him and his old lady liked to snort when they could afford it."

"Okay, and the Chupacabras are major dealers. But that is tenuous at best, Dehan."

"I know, but tenuous as it is, it is a damn sight more substantial than Bob's best lead at the time. Am I wrong?" She didn't wait for an answer. She knew she was right. She bulldozed on. "Now listen to this. The one thing that stands out about the killing of Adolfo and Mateo is the efficiency, right? The focus."

I nodded.

"Now go back to the killing of Karl and Christen. There is no frenzy with Karl, it is cool and efficient, and note: one quick stab to a vital organ to incapacitate, and then confirm the kill with a stab to the heart. *Exactly* the same as Adolfo and Mateo. Then, he goes in to Christen and he goes crazy, but he goes *focused* crazy. Remember, the ME said he had never seen anything like it."

"I remember. That struck me at the time."

"Fifteen or twenty blows, in rapid succession, all within a radius of four inches. Focus. I *know* it's not a lot, Stone, but you can smell it as clear as I can, this is the same killer."

I puffed out my cheeks and blew.

She shrugged. "Besides, it is all we got."

I nodded. "Which is probably why the case went cold. What do you suggest? The Chupacabras are not going to talk to us."

"What do *you* suggest?"

I made a face. "You won't like it. It has nothing to do with the angle you're looking at."

She shook her head. "You don't know that and neither do I because none of this makes any sense right now. Hit me."

"The boyfriend."

She blinked a few times to show her lack of enthusiasm. "Charlie."

"Charlie. He disappeared at the same time, remember?"

She shrugged. "I know, it *looks* significant. It's a hell of a coincidence, I agree, but at the time, Bob and Sanchez ruled him out."

I nodded. "They did, but still, that's where I would start."

"How? He disappeared."

"His mother. We go and talk to his mother."

CHAPTER 3

WE WENT AND HAD AN ABSURDLY EXPENSIVE LUNCH first, and then I insisted on taking in the Rubin Museum of Art, a place I had been threatening to take Dehan since we'd been married. She was always keen to explore different ideas and cultures, and I was pretty sure she would love the place, but that Sunday her comments on the Tibetan Buddhist Shrine Room were, "Uh-huh . . . ," her observation on the Gateway to Himalayan Art was, "Mm-hm . . . ," and her thoughts on Art and Politics in Tibetan Buddhism were, "Huh . . ." So after an hour, I suggested perhaps we could come back some other time, after we had spoken to Pamela Albright, Charlie's mother. She'd nodded with conviction.

"Yep, I'm down with that, Stone."

"Dehan, you owe me a Sunday."

"You got it, boss."

It was five thirty by the time we pulled up outside Pamela's large, handsome brownstone on East 127th. Two tasteful brass lamps flanked the large, highly polished mahogany door, and a large brass disk housed the original 1920s bell. A glance through the bay windows showed a number of what looked like genuine antiques. Unlike Amy's parents, Charlie Albright's mother was not poor.

Dehan rang the bell, and after a couple of minutes, the door opened. The woman who opened it was a bottle blonde, slim and well dressed, of average height and probably in her early fifties. She had once been attractive, but now relied on too much makeup and perfume to hide what age and alcohol were doing to her skin and her breath. Her smile suggested I could pour her a drink and Dehan could go play with the traffic. Dehan showed her her badge instead.

"I am Detective Dehan with the NYPD, ma'am, and this is Detective Stone. Are you Pamela Albright?"

She fingered a string of pearls at her neck. She didn't seem sure whether to be belligerent or accommodating and settled for incredulous as a compromise. "What on Earth does the NYPD want with me?"

I said, "We were wondering if we could ask you some questions about your son."

Her eyebrows shot up and she took half a step back. "*My son? Now? After six years?*"

I smiled understanding at her and said, "We run a cold-case unit out of the Forty-Third Precinct, Mrs. Albright, and we're taking another look at Charlie's case."

She frowned at me with slightly unfocused eyes, then turned to Dehan. Her frown was deepening. "What can you possibly hope to learn after all this time?"

I answered again. "We are not sure, but it is possible that Charlie's disappearance is related to another case. It's too early to say, but it might be a lead. May we come in?"

She considered us both a moment, then stepped back without saying anything.

The difference with the Redferns' house was striking. The layout was pretty much the same, with the broad staircase climbing the left wall of the substantial entrance hall, and a door on the right leading to a spacious, sunny living room and dining

room. But where the Redferns' house had been mauled and mutilated, and chopped into apartments without thought to its
elegant proportions and size, Pamela Albright's house had been
left intact, and had preserved all of its nineteenth-century
elegance.

White was obviously the thing with Pamela Albright. Her
drapes were white, the walls were white, the heavy, calico
armchairs and sofa were white, and the rugs on the floor, presumably to break the monotony, were cream. Both fireplaces, in the
living area and in the dining area, were white marble, and the
heavy dining table and the six chairs that surrounded it were also
white.

She gestured us to the two overstuffed chairs and lounged on
the sofa between us, angled slightly into the corner so as to look at
me. Dehan sat back, discreetly put her cell on record, and pulled a
notepad and pen from her jacket. Pamela pulled a cigarette from a
pack beside her on the sofa and lit up with a gold lighter that
looked like a Cartier. She inhaled deeply, watching me through
hooded eyes.

I said, "What can you tell me about Charlie's relationship
with Amy?"

"Amy?" She made an ugly face, with her very red mouth
drawn down at the sides. "She was a pretty little thing. A bit of a
hippie. Sweet and polite, little piece of nothing, really." She
breathed in sharply through her nose and her lids concealed her
eyes for a moment. "You see, Charlie had a problem."

Dehan glanced at her. I waited a moment, then asked, "What
kind of problem?"

"He was severely dyslexic, and dyspraxic. He was very bright.
Many dyslexic and dyspraxic children are. But it also made him
socially very awkward. He had huge difficulty relating to other
children, and though we wanted to send him to Gerald's prep
school, he didn't make it. It was terribly humiliating for Gerald."

Dehan said to her notebook, "Gerald?"

"My husband. He died when Charlie was just six."

Dehan raised an eyebrow at her notebook. "Aged six, he had already humiliated his father. Put that in your Oedipal pipe and smoke it."

Pamela turned bodily to scowl at Dehan, who focused hard on making notes on her pad. I said, "So he went to public school?"

"I had little choice," she said coldly. "With Gerald gone, I went to pieces. He was my rock, my strength. He was a banker, you know? He made sure the house was paid for and we had a generous income, but it was the loss of that strength, his presence, you understand?"

She frowned at me, as though I might not understand. I nodded to reassure her that I did, so she went on.

"My family rallied at first, as did his, but people are fickle, Mr. Stone, aren't they? When they see that you are mourning in your own way, not in theirs, or at their pace, they grow impatient. Poor Charlie grew very attached to my mother and my sister after Gerald left, and he missed them when they went too."

Dehan looked at her sharply and raised an eyebrow. "They . . . *went?*"

"Back to Miami."

I scratched my chin. "So all of this must have aggravated Charlie's dyspraxia."

"Of course, the stress and the anxiety played havoc with him. I often wonder if I could have done more to help him. I should have done more, I know . . ."

"But it sounds as though he was able to relate to Amy."

She leaned forward. "She was the *only* person he could relate to. It was distressing. Her parents were these hippie types . . ." She paused, gazing at the window. "They weren't really even interesting enough to be hippies. They didn't bake lentil bread or grow pot or anything like that. They just didn't wash very often, and he, the father, had his hair matted into long strands. I think he did it intentionally. She seemed inoffensive enough, the mother, Cristina . . . ?"

"Christen."

"Yes, that's it, but I didn't like Charlie going over there. I always worried he'd catch something. And I'm sure the other parents used to look at her and Charlie and call them the odd couple."

"So they were friends for a long time."

"From the beginning. She was a sweet child, like a little fairy. White, white skin, little white face with blue, blue eyes and platinum hair. Skinny little arms and legs, always dressed in clothes that somebody had passed on, so they never quite fit. Sometimes she'd go into school and her face hadn't been washed, or nobody had brushed her hair. So Charlie would ask me if she could come home after school, and he would wash her face, or insist that we give her a bath, and comb her hair for her. He cared for her as though she were his own sister."

"He had no other friends?"

She sucked on her cigarette, drew the smoke down deep, and spoke with little clouds puffing from her mouth as she crushed the butt in the ashtray. "She was the only one who didn't torment him. She was nice to him, and they stuck together. Soon the other kids learned to leave them alone. By the time she was ten or eleven years old, I think she spent as much time here as she did at her own place. They used to play that I was going to adopt her. Poor child. Perhaps I should have."

She laughed and I smiled. She swung her legs off the sofa and stood.

"I can feel dehydration threatening. Can I offer either of you a drink? I am sorely in need of a gin and tonic."

We told her she couldn't, and she made her way with the careful grace and dignity of a habitual drunk to a collection of bottles on a sideboard in the dining area. She spoke as she built the drink. "Of course, I imagine that they started experimenting with sex in his room. And I wasn't sure *what* to do about that. I mean, he was so shy, and so awkward to talk to. If I had attempted to broach a subject like that with him . . . ." She laughed out loud as she returned to the sofa and sat. "A child of that age can get pregnant, you know."

Dehan had put down her pen and was frowning hard at Pamela. "So what did you do?"

"I had Fettuccini . . ."

I shook my head. "Fettuccini?"

She laughed again. "Oh, her name is Fernanda, but it seems to me such an absurd name for a woman that I call her Fettuccini. She is the woman who does for me. She's been with me for years, God love her. I had her go to the clinic and get leaflets and things, and a box of condoms, and I had her leave them all in his room. The poor child never got pregnant, so it must have worked."

A silence fell on the room. My mind went back to the filthy bedroom Bob had found six years ago, the dirty sheets, the unwashed underwear on the floor, the closed drapes and the fetid air, the moldy cornflakes under the bed. I tried to see it all in the context of this little fairy, the sweet little hippie with Charlie bathing her and combing her hair.

I drew breath. "So, did they have plans? Were they in love, engaged, planning to live together, get married . . . ?"

She pouted and spread her hands. "I don't know. *Obviously* they didn't do well at school. They barely scraped into community college. I don't even remember what they were studying. He was studying IT, I think. They didn't really care, as long as they were together. That was the big thing for them. She might have been studying English literature, I honestly don't remember. They both loved poetry, and they used to read *The Lord of the Rings* to each other. Oh, and she was a Christian, always talking about early Christianity, Jesus, and Antioch. My *God*, it was tedious. But they never shared their plans with me. We didn't discuss things as a family. They decided and I paid."

I sat forward, with my elbows on my knees and my hands clasped, as though I were praying. "Pamela, by the time they disappeared, was she spending more time here than at home, would you say?"

"God, yes. She was practically living here. He used to sneak her up to his room at night, thinking I didn't notice. In the end, she was spending days on end here before going back home for a day, two at the most, then coming back here. Can't say I blamed her."

"And the day he disappeared . . ."

Her face became drawn. "It's all a bit of a blur, to tell you the truth. It was very traumatic."

"I can imagine, but if you can help us to go over it again, we may be able to find out what happened to him, even . . ." I shrugged and left the words hanging.

She gave a dry little laugh. "He ain't coming home, Detective Stone. I don't know what got into him, but he ain't coming back." She sighed, pulled another cigarette from her pack, and lit up. Smoke trailed from her open mouth. "He came home late on the Saturday night. I remember that. He was alone. I was already in bed. But next morning, I asked him where Amy was. He said he didn't know."

I said, "Did that strike you as unusual?"

She waved her cigarette in the air. "He was always so surly and sullen. Never gave me a civil answer. I thought nothing of it. I do remember it had been a very hectic weekend. It seemed everybody was coming or going or tramping in or tramping out . . ."

"So she was here part of the weekend. Was she here Saturday?"

She rolled her eyes, groaned, then laughed. "Like I say. It was a chaotic weekend. People coming and going." She raised an eyebrow at me. "I haven't always been single, you know." She sighed when I didn't smile. "I am pretty sure she was here, on and off on Saturday, but what time she left, or came back . . ." She spread her hands. "Sorry. I'm a bad girl."

Dehan made a question with her face and showed it to me. I ignored it and asked Pamela, "You said you're sure Charlie isn't coming back. Where do you think he is, Pamela?"

She sucked on her cigarette, and I saw a small tremble. I saw tears in her eyes, and she shook her head, reaching quickly for a handkerchief to dab at her nose. "I think he's dead." She shrugged. "I wasn't the best mom in the world, but I wasn't the worst. I never hurt him. Never even smacked him when he was small. He always had everything he wanted. This was a home for him and for Amy. If he was alive, he would have called. He would have called to say he was okay." She gave a sudden, wet laugh. "He would have called to ask for money."

The laugh died away. She tapped ash even though there was none on the tip. "I don't know what happened that weekend. But whatever it was, it was bad. And I know it cost poor Amy her life, and I think Charlie went shortly after. Maybe he couldn't be without her. That's possible."

I thought about that. It was certainly possible, but it was also unlikely that in six years, his body wouldn't have shown up somewhere. I put my hands on my knees and made to stand, but then stopped and frowned at her, dabbing at her nose with her handkerchief. I smiled. "Change of season, gets you every time."

She returned the smile with a small laugh. "Oh, no. I'm fine. It's just the talk, it has brought it all back."

She still had the handkerchief to her nose. I glanced around the room, looking for the box. I didn't see it. I said, "Do you still do it? It's an expensive habit."

She kind of collapsed, sighed, and laughed all at the same time. "You are determined to drag me through the mire today, aren't you, Detective Stone? I did *a lot* of it at one time. It has a way of making you feel invincible and indestructible. It also has a way of making you crazy and burning a hole right through your bank account. After Charlie disappeared, several friends performed what I believe is known as an intervention on me. They made me see that if I had not been out of my mind all weekend, I might just have been able to save Charlie. So I stopped." She held up her glass of gin and tonic. "This I am hanging on to until Charlie comes home. If he ever does, I'll jack it in."

I nodded a few times. "Who sold you the coke, back in the day?"

"Oh my god, really?" She thought for a moment. "His name was . . . *Felix*. We were never what you'd call friends, but he was at all the parties and he supplied to *a lot* of people. I mean, we were not the crème de la crème of New York society, but we were on the fringe, he had some pretty influential clients, and he was making a great deal of money."

"You still in touch?"

"No! And I *really* don't want to be."

"Don't worry." I smiled. "I don't want you to be either. Who can we talk to about tracking him down?"

She thought about it for a minute, then shook her head. "I don't know. I really, honestly, don't know."

Her eyes were big and wet and scared, and I didn't push. I stood. "Thank you, Pamela. You have been very helpful. We'll let you know if we get any news. We'll see ourselves out . . ."

As we stepped into the hall, I glanced back and saw her at the dresser in the dining room again, mixing herself a strong one.

Dehan took the stoop three steps at a time and stood looking at my burgundy beast. I followed, she tossed me the keys, and I went around to the driver's side. She leaned her chin on her arms on the roof and stared at me. I said, "What?"

She frowned and her voice was serious. "I have ruined your Sunday, and I think the least I can do is cook you a sirloin and get you a bottle of wine. You deserve it."

Scan the QR code below to purchase THE FALL MOON.
Or go to: righthouse.com/the-fall-moon